ABOUT THIS BOOK

The third annual Havenwood Falls Short Story Anthology brings all-new holiday romances to warm you up on these cold winter nights.

Prepare your warm drink, grab your favorite blanket, and settle in for a heartwarming and romantic read of several short stories about some of your favorite Havenwood Falls families.

Join the Blackstone witch hunters as they try to connect with their ancestors; find out if Curtis Parker, a gay witch who just can't seem to find love in his small hometown, can get lucky when a leprechaun walks into his office; help Rusty, the sexy wolf-shifter ranger, find out what happened to his human bride, Sherry, who literally disappeared in thin air; find out if Old Man Mills can learn his lesson and become less of a Scrooge; go back in time to the 1980s with the Kasun family; and wrap it up where it all began, with the moroi vampires, Michaela and Xandru, who just might finally get their wedding day—until the biggest blizzard of the decade blows in.

As always with Havenwood Falls, several of your other favorite characters make appearances as they all come together for the holidays.

These short stories are all about love, friends, and family, brought to you by *USA Today* and Amazon bestselling and award-winning authors in the Havenwood Falls Collective.

Authors in this anthology include:

Kristie Cook
E.J. Fechenda
Morgan Wylie
Kallie Ross
Amy Hale
Susan Burdorf

HAVENWOOD FALLS SHORT STORY ANTHOLOGY 2020

HAVENWOOD FALLS COLLECTIVE

DON'T MISS OUT!

Stay up to date at www.HavenwoodFalls.com

Subscribe to our reader group and receive free stories and more!

REUNITED

BY MORGAN WYLIE

A Blackstone Witch Hunter Short Story

"Every year there seems to be more and more Christmas decoration boxes," Brock, the eldest Blackstone son, said, heaving a stack of boxes down a narrow stairway from the attic in their Havenwood Heights family home.

"Well, of course there is. We add to the collection *every year*," Macy, his sister, said with exuberance. She ran back up after her brother descended to get yet more boxes, her light blond hair flying in the air behind her. Brice, the youngest son, ran up from the main floor to retrieve the next pile from the attic. Up until a few years ago, most of the family believed Brice to be an anomaly—the only male witch hunter—but when Macy left home and discovered a group of rogue witch hunters, she realized they'd been wrong and purposely kept in the dark.

"Yeah, Mom, I think we have plenty of decorations. No more this year, huh?" Brice playfully shouted down the stairs.

"Oh, Brice, quit complaining," his mom and matriarch of the Blackstone witch hunters, Lilith, shouted up at him in return.

"My sentiments exactly," Macy added with a bit of playful snark as she followed him with her own stack piled in her hands. From

1

behind, a pine garland was unexpectedly wrapped around her neck like a scarf. She stumbled, almost tipping her pile.

"Whoa! Macy, hold on," Reggie, their dad, shouted as he moved quickly to steady her, grabbing a few of her boxes. Reginald Blackstone ran the Stone Falls Winery and oversaw all the Blackstone business ventures including Soothing Sips tasting bar, NamaStays Inn, and more recently, Blackstone Brothers Micro Brews.

Macy spit out a few artificial pine needles from her mouth and loosened the garland from her neck. "Thanks a lot, Brock." Sarcasm dripped from her words. "This thing itches!"

"Why did you choose to wear it then?" Brock asked with mocking innocence.

"Haha, very funny." She pointed back at him. "Dad, he tried to use Christmas against me . . . to harm me! Who does that?" Macy asked with feigned shock.

Brock set his boxes down and quickly scooped a laughing Macy up and threw her over his shoulder. As she beat at his back, there was a knock at the door.

"I'll get it," Brock practically dropped her on the couch and strode toward the door.

"Is he expecting someone?" Lilith asked, her brow furrowed.

"I don't think so." Macy shrugged, then adjusted her clothing as she got herself up from the couch.

"I am, though!" Brice shouted, then ran toward the door.

"From the look on his face, I'd guess Sunny was joining us this evening," Reggie surmised with a twinkle in his eyes.

"Wise deduction, Father," Macy said with her best detective voice and began to pull out boxes of ornaments marked FRAGILE and set them aside.

"Macy, set all those Blackstone heirloom ornaments up on the kitchen bar top, so nothing happens to them while we get the rest of this organized." Lilith gestured to the chaos of open boxes exploding with green garlands, white batting for snow backdrops, village houses, and bright red and green ornaments of all shapes and sizes.

"Sure thing, Mom. I love these old ornaments. We should archive pictures of each for a scrapbook or something, so we always remember them in case something happens to them. Wouldn't that be cool?" Macy beamed with the thought.

"That's a great idea, dear, but would you have time to do that in between college at Sun & Moon Academy and working at NamaStays Inn on your off days? Don't push it . . . but maybe it could be a continuous project that your brothers help with, too." Reggie set down a box marked MANTLE by the fireplace.

"What is Dad volunteering us for?" Brock asked, walking back into the main living area followed by Brice, who held Sunny's hand, her face lit up like the sunshine she embodied.

"Oh, just world domination, stuff like that," Macy replied casually.

"Sweet, I'm ready. Bring it on!" Brice said with his fist in the air. They all laughed.

"Your sister thought it would be cool to catalog the ancestor's Christmas ornaments in a scrapbook," Dad explained.

"We'd want to make sure to store it online, too, you know, in case something happened to the book. It wouldn't really mean anything to save the memories if they went up in smoke with the actual ornaments," Brock grimly stated.

"That's a good point, Brock," Lilith acknowledged from behind the beautiful blue spruce tree they had cut down from the land behind the vineyard. She walked around, surveying branches and trimming unwanted ones.

"Are you giving the tree a haircut, Mom?" Brice asked, confused.

"Of course. I do it every year. I try to make it as even as I can before we start."

"Have you never seen Mom do that?" Macy asked in surprise.

He shrugged. "I guess not."

"We're being rude. Hello, Sunny. We're so glad you could join us tonight to decorate the tree," Lilith said, changing the subject.

Sunny had already made herself comfortable sitting cross-legged on the couch. Her golden curls were piled high on her head, but it did not diminish the smile on her face as she watched the family's interaction.

"Yes, hello, Sunny. Can I get you a holiday beverage?" Reggie asked, heading into the kitchen.

"I'd love some eggnog! I'd never had that before I came to your house." Her face lit up even more, if it was possible.

"You got it! Anyone else need a refill?"

"I'll get mine and help you, Dad." Brock headed to the kitchen as well. "You have to test our newest holiday microbrew and let me know what you think."

"We haven't decided on a name yet, but we're thinking of calling it the Mountain Top Ale," Brice shouted back at them. "It tastes a bit like pine . . . allegedly," he added.

Since graduating from the Sun and Moon Academy—the private high school—Brice had begun to work with Brock on their microbrews as a covert side gig. Brice was still underage, so he did most of the marketing and behind-the-scenes work while Brock worked with the brews. He had considered attending the same college as Macy this past fall, but after learning how challenging it was for her and her friends, he didn't feel he was ready; and when Sunny confirmed it with her Seer gifts, he chose to wait until next summer to make that decision.

"Sounds fantastic. What a great idea to have a holiday ale!" The family had been in the wine business as far back as they could remember, but Reggie was proud of his sons and supported their growing expansion.

"Macy, where's Gallad tonight?" Sunny asked as she gratefully accepted the mug, then closed her eyes and enjoyed her first sip as if it were from heaven.

"He's spending time with his own family tonight. They also have a tradition of decorating their tree Thanksgiving weekend. He'll drop by a little later, and then I'll go spend a little time with his family, too." Gallad Augustine was from one of the oldest witch families in Havenwood Falls and also Macy's fiancé.

"That's so nice," Sunny said wistfully.

The family decorated and chatted for the next couple hours, sipping wine and eggnog. The fire crackled and popped in the large fireplace while Christmas music played softly in the background.

"Okay, everyone, now that all the ancestor ornaments have been hung, the time has come for the tree topper. Who has it?" Lilith asked, looking around the room. Everyone glanced at each other and then began to search through boxes. "This is our most valued heirloom ornament. It should have been over on the counter with the others." Her voice was full of panic.

"I found it! It's okay." Brock pulled out a beautiful black velvet box from inside a larger packing box. He carefully brought it over to his mom and handed it to her.

"Thank you, Brock." She uncharacteristically paused. "Would you like to do the honors?"

"Really? But I'm not a hunter," he replied.

"No, but you are our son and a Blackstone. We want you to position it this year," she replied and lovingly placed her hand on his arm.

He paused. The moment filled with emotion. He nodded and opened the box. Brock pulled out a hollow wooden ball. The exterior was intricately carved in a lacework pattern in order to see the white crystal encased within it, suspended by an iron rod. Even though they'd seen the ornament every year, still they were awed at the sight.

"Wow, it's so pretty!" Sunny expressed. "I can feel the elemental magic coming from it. It's from the Falls, right?" She scrunched her face in concentration. "I'm trying to remember what you told me last year."

"Yes, it's magic is from the waterfall of Havenwood Falls itself," Lilith stated.

"I'm so excited!" Macy said, jumping to her feet and moving in closer to the tree. Everyone followed her lead. Then they heard the door open and close at the front of the house and paused.

"Did I miss it?" came Gallad's voice from the entry as he made his way to the family.

"Nope, not yet," Macy said, cutting through her family to grab his hand and bring him to stand with her near the hearth of the fireplace. "We are just about to light it."

"This is my favorite part," he said gleefully. Everyone said a quick hello to him, then their focus went back to the tree.

"Are we ready?" Lilith asked as she twisted an ornament lower on the tree and straightened another. "I think they're all in position."

"First the lighting of the Christmas lights!" Brice interjected. "We need to do that first for the full effect."

"Go for it, Brice," Brock and Macy replied.

Brice counted down, "3, 2, 1."

He plugged in the lights, and the tree lit the room.

"It's beautiful!" Sunny whispered, and everyone agreed with her.

"Now for the piece de resistance," Brock added with flare and steadied the tree topper in his hands. "Ready?"

"I wish the Blackstones from the past could see how we have honored their traditions and, of course, added our own. I would especially love to see Great-Great-Grandma Marie, the one who helped settle this place in the 1800's," Macy said with longing. "I mean, we wouldn't be here without her."

Suddenly Sunny inhaled sharply.

"You can!" She clapped her hands and gleefully looked around the room to find each of them staring at her, confused. "You can have them here—the Blackstones who have passed on." Sunny had Seer gifts, but they were unpredictable.

"What do you mean, Sunny?" Lilith asked with suspicion, gesturing for Brock to pause putting the topper on the tree.

"I don't remember her name . . . Hope, maybe? She can contact the dead and summon them to this side of the veil, right? Maybe she could call them over to visit for a little bit!"

"You mean, Harper Sinclair? Can she do that?" Macy asked with hopeful wonder.

"I bet she totally could!" Brice jumped up, putting his hand on Sunny's shoulder.

"Now, hold on," Lilith interrupted. "I think this might be more up her aunt Eloise's alley. But I would need to talk to the Court about that first—if Eloise is willing to do it, that is."

"Would they be open to that, Lilith?" Reggie asked.

"I don't know for sure, but they just might."

"Once you have permission, Brice and I could set up a protection spell. I could ask Grandma Mathilde to make sure I use the right one to keep out any unwanted visitors," Gallad offered.

"Ryne could help. He's been practicing his witch side, too," Brice said, referring to Ryne Calloway, half phoenix and half witch, and also Hollis Blackstone's boyfriend.

"That could be amazing," Macy said. "Just think! We could ask questions about the past—Brice, that could be especially helpful for you to talk with Great-Great-Grandpa Judson, don't you think?"

"Absolutely. I'm kinda stabbing in the dark, trying to learn how to mix my magic side with my hunter. They might have some insight into what their children dealt with before they were suppressed." Brice's expression was a mix of hope and also concern at the last part of his statement.

"You made your choice and you are doing an amazing job, Brice. Don't you forget it," Sunny said adamantly. He reached his arm around her shoulder and pulled her in tight.

"Then it is settled. I will approach the Court on this matter. Let's keep this just between us for now until we know for sure. I don't want word to get out the hunters are trying to raise their dead. Someone is bound to think we're raising an army to take over Havenwood Falls or something asinine." Lilith shook her head in exasperation.

"You got it, Mom," Brock agreed.

"Can we hold off lighting the heirloom ornaments until then? We could do it all together, at NamaStays Inn, since that is where it all began for us here in Havenwood Falls," Macy suggested.

"Great idea, Mace. I think that sounds lovely," her dad replied, and the rest of them agreed.

"You'll get your chance," Lilith said to Brock as he placed the tree topper back in its box. He nodded with a smile.

Macy clapped her hands together in front of her face. "I'm so excited this could happen! I'll need to plan what I want to ask Marie."

"You can think about it in the car. I told my parents we would head their way in just a little bit." Gallad reached for Macy's hand.

"Of course! Mom, anything you need us to do before we go to the Augustines'?" Macy asked, pulling Gallad behind her as she grabbed her coat off the back of a dining chair.

"No, thank you. We'll just clean up here. Gallad, tell your mother hello from me."

"Have fun you two!" Reggie offered, clapping Gallad on the back.

The remaining Blackstones cleaned up the mess and simply enjoyed the ambiance of the tree, their decorations, and the eggnog.

❄

After a week of deliberation with the Court of the Sun and the Moon, Lilith was granted the petition to approach Eloise Sinclair. Macy spent all her free time helping to organize the event they scheduled for the middle of December. She and Aunt Letti planned for even more Christmas decorations at NamaStays so everything would look perfect.

When the day finally arrived, Macy, Brice, and Sunny drove in to town for final supplies and decorations at the shops around the town square. Macy checked in with Eloise at her shop, Into the Mystic New Age Books and Gifts, to see if she had any last minute preparation needs, and to pick up candles. She sent Brice and Sunny with a list to Howe's Herbal Shoppe and then to Fairy Tale Florists to get the fresh wreaths and garlands she had ordered. Many of the town's people were carrying about their day, none the wiser of what the Blackstones were about to do. They all met back at the car with their boxes and bags.

"Hey, Blackstones!" A beautiful woman in black combat boots and a matching leather jacket strode toward them. With long black hair flowing behind her, she stood out amongst the surrounding red, white, and green holiday decor.

Macy waved. "Hey Hollis! I wondered if we were going to bump into you before tonight."

Hollis was a Blackstone from the rogue side of the family led by Dante Blackstone, who believed they should be the dominant race as witch hunters and eradicate the world of witches. She was Dante's daughter who turned against him and became a resident of Havenwood Falls a year and a half ago. Hollis wanted to coexist with the witches and other species and finally settle down.

"I've never been a part of a spirit channeling before." Hollis paused and uncharacteristically bit her lip. "Actually, if I'm honest, I'm a bit nervous. What if they aren't happy that I'm here with you all?"

Macy turned Hollis toward her. "Are you kidding? They will be ecstatic to meet you and know how you've overcome your

8

upbringing. We might have to tell them the story, but it will be okay. You'll see."

Hollis grabbed Macy's arm and tugged her along the sidewalk. "Let's grab coffee and some of Coffee Haven's famous festive treats for tonight. It'll be getting dark soon, and I need to pick up Ryne when we're done, then I'll meet you back at NamaStays tonight, right?"

"Mmm . . . Eggnog lattes. Yes, please!" Sunny said with longing, to which Brice laughed.

"You got it!" he told her, wrapping his arm around her.

They all walked in peaceful silence, enjoying the festive atmosphere of the snow-covered town. Holiday music was magically piped throughout the square, thanks to the local Luna Coven, the entire way to Coffee Haven.

After they received their goodies, Gallad walked in and met them with his bad-boy smile. "You all ready to go? Hollis, I want to go over the—" he looked around at the nearby patrons to make sure he didn't say anything witchy around the humans— "recipe for tonight with Ryne and Brice. Will he be shortly behind us?"

"Yes, I'll get him now and meet you all at the vineyard. He's been practicing his . . ." She also paused conspiratorially. ". . . that side of him more than usual. It's cute. He wants to help. And I'll help decorate or whatever else needs to be done while you're doing that," she added.

"Okay, we'll meet you there!"

"Lilith, where do you want the rest of these decorations to go?" Hollis asked later at NamaStays Inn at the Vineyard. She and Sunny each had their hands full of extra garland and vines of red berries. The smell of pine was deliciously intoxicating.

"I want some with lights to go around the banister leading upstairs, but other than that, go ahead and put them wherever you think they would look good. Make sure there are decorations and a wreath outside on the porch, too," Lilith directed.

They both nodded and went to work, wrapping garland with tiny white lights along the staircase banister.

Macy placed candles around the room for decoration while Gallad, Ryne, and Brice arranged specific candles as well as salt around the interior of the room for protection. They chanted an approved spell under their breath.

Lilith and Aunt Letti perfected the decorations on the tree, while Uncle Tranner, Letti's dragon-shifter husband, and Brock chopped wood outside for the barrel fires in front of the inn as well as their neighboring winery. Only a few people rented cabins for the holidays this year, but several locals and tourists enjoyed their wine by heat lamps under the white lights of the big patio, at least until the snow fell again.

"So why did we decide to do this here instead of up at the big house?" Hollis asked anyone who would answer.

"We felt like this would be the strongest location for the magic as many of our ancestors had either built this or lived here before the big house was finished. They had more invested here in this ground, literally, so it could be an easier point of entry but also a more familiar place for them to visit. At least in theory," Macy said with a shrug.

"It's possible it might not work at all. So keep your hopes realistic, Macy," Eva, her grandmother, said, bringing reality back to her.

Macy frowned but then smiled, despite her grandmother's negativity. "I know, but I believe it will work. Have a little faith, Grandma."

"Honestly, I am uncertain if Eloise can handle this—it might be too many for her to channel. Bringing a soul across is one thing, but bringing an entire family across is another."

"So then have a little Christmas faith! All things are possible, especially here in this town. We know this." Macy placed her last candle, then stood back.

"Okay, everyone, watch this. I went a little new school this year for the decor candles, but this is actually safer for the inn," Macy announced.

"What on earth are you going on about?" Eva questioned.

"Watch . . ." Macy held her hand out. The candles all simultaneously sprung to life with a soft yellow flickering glow. "They're LED candles. I can set them on a timer, and they won't burn the place down. Win-win!" She piled her long blond hair on top of her head in a sloppy knot.

"So it's not real fire?" her grandmother asked.

"Right! You can touch them. They won't burn down or out. I guess the batteries could die, but they are guaranteed for like a lot of hours. Cool, huh?"

"Very pretty, Macy," Sunny said with a big grin, looking around.

"I love it," Aunt Letti added with a reassuring smile.

"Well done, Macy," Hollis acknowledged. Lilith and Eva also agreed.

Finally finished with the decorations, Sunny turned on the stereo. Soft holiday music played in the background. Hollis brought out a tray filled with mugs of eggnog and her Coffee Haven treats. Brock, Reggie, and Tranner came in from outside, shaking off their coats and stomping the snow off their boots.

"We are just waiting on Gallad, Ryne, and Brice to finish up, and Eloise should be here soon," Lilith stated to everyone anxiously standing around.

Macy looked out the window. "It's snowing again. At least there won't be people on the patio much longer."

"Well, Gallad reassured me the protection spell they placed would also keep out prying eyes, or even just those in the wrong place at the wrong time," Aunt Letti explained.

"Good. Everyone has thoroughly thought through this process," Dad acknowledged.

"Indeed," Eva said, sitting rigidly, studying various ornaments.

The door opened abruptly, and three men walked heavily through the door, stomping and shaking off as much snow from outside as possible.

"Finished?" Macy asked with enthusiasm.

"Yes. We positioned everything inside earlier, then we completed it outside with a final spell. I believe we should be ready to go . . . assuming I did my grandma's spell right," Gallad said with humor. He gave Macy a quick innocent kiss on the top of her head.

"I'm sure it's perfect," she said with a smile.

"Get a room, you two!" Brice said with mock gagging gestures.

"Brice!" Lilith said sharply.

"Is Ms. Sinclair here yet?" Ryne interrupted, rubbing his hands in front of the newly built fire.

"No—"

A knock at the door theatrically suggested otherwise.

Being closest, Brock opened it. A flurry of snow ushered in a woman swathed in a cloak and a multitude of colorful scarves up to her head.

"Welcome, Eloise. Please come inside," Brock said in the most gentlemanly way.

"Thank you. I hope I'm not late, although it's no secret I like to make an entrance," she said, winking at Brock then handing him her outerwear.

"Not at all. You're right on time, in fact," Aunt Letti said, ushering the woman into the center of the room. It wasn't a large space, but the foyer was large enough for them all to comfortably fit.

"Thank you for coming, Eloise," Lilith added. "We appreciate you doing this for us."

Eloise Sinclair shook the snow off her auburn hair to reveal tinted white highlights and looked around the room with a warm smile. "I am happy to do this for you, but you also need to know that it may not work. Spirits on the other side can be fickle. They may not want to be disturbed. Or they may come all too easy and make it difficult to leave. But those are usually agitated spirits not at rest. Hopefully, none of your family feel that way," Eloise said with an uneasy tinge to her tone and a nervous laugh.

The atmosphere in the room thickened. The Blackstones looked around at each other, an unspoken question in their eyes . . . until it wasn't.

"Can Dante get through, Lilith?" Hollis quietly asked the question no one else seemed to want to ask.

"No . . . no . . . there's no way. At least, I have been reassured there should be no way for him to," she responded, her voice holding an element of uncertainty that her expression showed even she was uncomfortable with.

"You don't seem so certain. Mom," Brock hesitantly questioned, "maybe we shouldn't go through with this?"

"Sunny, do you see anything, you know, about this event?"

Brice asked her quietly. Ever since she'd revealed her abilities as a Seer as well as a hunter, he tried not to push her. She usually volunteered information when she felt it pertinent. But this was important.

She pinched her brows for a brief second, then shook her head. "All I see are several different ancestors here with us. So it works, Ms. Sinclair!"

Eloise nodded gratefully. "Then we are agreed. I, too, see that. All right. Let's do this then. Witches, is your spell set?" She shook her hands out with a flourish like a conductor preparing her symphony.

"Yes," Gallad responded as representative.

"Can I get you something to drink first, Eloise?" Uncle Tranner asked.

"Some eggnog would be lovely." She reached into her bag, pulled out a small flask, and handed it to him with a wink. "Put a couple splashes of that in with it, would you?"

He nodded with a knowing smirk.

"Okay, witches, I want you positioned at the three points of a triangle around me. Everyone else in a loose circle within the perimeter of their spell. Don't step outside it; otherwise, you won't be able to see what is happening within the circle. Is that correct, Gallad?"

He nodded at her.

Everyone moved into position. "Is there anything we should be doing to be helpful?" Macy asked.

"Think of your ancestors. Think of the ones you wish to contact the most. Visualize them crossing over into this room. If you believe, it will help the process be more smoothly accepted," she encouraged as she pulled out of her bag a candle she brought and lit it. Eloise then gracefully knelt in the center of the room, laid out her notepad and candle, closed her eyes, and invitingly extended her arms, palms up. A low hum came from deep in her chest. Then she began to move her hand and pencil. "Call out the first names of who we are inviting."

"Marie Blackstone," Macy called out first.

"Judson Carter Blackstone," Brice confidently added.

"Cessily Blackstone," Eva said.

"Hank Blackstone." Aunt Letti smiled and nodded at Eva. Previously, they had discussed wanting to meet the pair.

"Good, let's start there," Eloise said breathlessly as she wrote their names over and over on her notepad. As a spiritual writer, it enabled her to connect to those she channeled by writing something to anchor them to the mortal realm. She gasped and whispered, "They're coming."

The Blackstones and the extended members of their family glanced nervously at each other. Sunny bounced on the balls of her feet in excited anticipation next to Brice. Lilith and Reggie held hands, standing close to, but still within, the circle's edge, along with her mother, Eva. Aunt Letti and Uncle Tranner stood near Macy, who rubbed her hands nervously next to Gallad. Brock, Ryne, and Hollis stood at the other end of the room. As a precaution, the council had thought it best to have everyone near a magic wielder in case something should go wrong.

Images of people in strange attire, clothing of farmers in the late 1800s, began to wink in and out until fully visible and ghostly transparent.

"Grandmother!" both Aunt Letti and Eva gasped in unison. They were both the granddaughters of Marie Blackstone, but from different mothers, Aunt Letti from Janella and Eva from Rhea. Aunt Letti screeched and began to run toward the apparition, forgetting she would not be tangible. Marie had passed away in 2000, the same year Macy had been born.

"Judson's here too! Oh, and Hank!" Brice shouted after having researched old albums and records the Blackstone family kept.

"Cessily?" Eva asked hesitantly at the newest soul who had slowly appeared in the room. The ghost simply nodded her head and smiled. She studied everyone in the room with a mix of pride and sadness in her eyes.

"Why is she not speaking?" Lilith asked the void.

"Sometimes, if the spirits are very old, it's harder to pull them across, or they may lose the ability to communicate with the current world," Eloise explained through her focus as she continued to write their names.

"We have spoken on the other side," Marie interjected with a wispy sounding voice, "and she is current on most of what has happened to her children—since I have passed over, at least."

Hank, Cessily's husband and Marie's father, went to stand by her and held her hand. "It has been most troubling for her to not see all her children together, but she understands they made their choices. She was not completely surprised to hear Dante had chosen the path he had, but we both were disappointed."

"There are other Blackstones. Should we wait for them?" Aunt Letti asked.

"We are the strongest. The others chose us to represent them," Marie shared.

"It can be a challenge to cross to this side of the veil," Eloise added.

"Cessily?" Hollis took a step forward to be acknowledged. "I'm Hollis . . . Hollis Cessily Blackstone, Dante's daughter and your granddaughter. He spoke of you and held a softness in his heart toward you. I think, in part, that's why he named me after you. Anyway, I'm here. I wanted you to know," Hollis said, uncharacteristically hesitant. Ryne gripped her hand.

Cessily moved swiftly to hover in front of Hollis, surveying her face. She smiled through ghostly tears running from her eyes. Cessily held her hands just outside Hollis's face, as if cupping her cheeks between them. Hollis could feel the warmth and love radiating from her ghostly grandmother and smiled in return.

"This is so amazing!" Sunny said in semi-hushed tones to Brice at her side.

The spirits moved around the room and chatted with everyone there. So much was to be said with too little time. Marie and Judson made their way to Macy and Gallad.

"Marie, I know I was too young when you passed, but I feel your presence with me often, like we are connected somehow. I've always wanted to meet you," Macy admitted.

"The connection is mutual, Macy. We don't have much time, but know I am always with you in your heart. I want to say something to you and Gallad both, as you are the first witch-hunter pairing since Judson and myself. The connection is amazing when you find your soulmate, but because of the strain on the conflicting magic within, our children suffered early on." Marie paused and looked sad.

"Brice, you should hear this too," Judson said, waving Brice to join them. "It will affect where you are now."

Brice nodded and joined them. "I was hoping to have a chance to talk with you about this. Thank you."

Others quieted down to hear their words as well.

"We have been concerned for Brice, but he seems to be handling himself pretty well," Lilith added, gripping Reggie's hand.

"Go ahead, Marie, continue please," Judson said politely, placing his transparent hand encouragingly at her lower back.

She smiled up at him, his stature much taller than her own. "Yes, Brice, I'm glad you are doing so well. Our children were younger when they started showing signs of conflict between the hunter and the witch magic within them. We had never heard of it happening that way before and had no one to advise us on how to guide them. What we did do with the help of some of the Havenwood Falls witches—some you still know, such as Gallad's grandmother Mathilde Augustine and Saundra Beaumont—we regretted later on. We hold no ill will toward those who helped us. No one knew any differently at the time, and we didn't want the children—not only ours, but those to come—to suffer." Marie paused again and looked at all those before them as that trait could have spread throughout any of the hunters among them.

"What did you do?" Brice asked, leaning in with rapt attention.

"We suppressed and bound their magic and allowed the hunter to take dominance," she said, her tone full of sadness. "We unknowingly kept them from a part of who they could have been."

Marie looked to Brice with a big smile, then gestured toward him. "Brice is proof that the two, witch hunter and witch, could find a way to coexist, albeit I'm sure not without its challenges. Am I right, Brice?"

He nodded. "Daily challenges. But the more I embrace each side and allow them space to flex their power, whether that be practicing active magic or using my abilities to sense other witches, then the more both parts seem to . . ." He mentally searched for the word. "Coexist, as you said."

"Very good, Brice." Judson attempted to pat Brice on the back of his shoulder, but his hand simply slipped right through. He sheepishly adjusted his cowboy hat, then put his hands into his trouser pockets.

"Thank you, Grandpa Judson, I appreciate that," Brice said with a reassuring smile.

"Grandpa . . . I like the sound of that. I never got to hear those words when I lived. Thank you." Judson smiled in return.

"Back to Macy and Gallad," Marie said. "I know your future is still before you and you have many choices and obstacles to face, but you can overcome all of them if you work together as a team. Judson and I have been a team since the very beginning, and we overcame some big challenges."

She smiled up at Judson, her eyes full of love. Cessily and Hank joined Marie and Judson. These were the ones who had paved a way and given the opportunity to the Havenwood Falls Blackstones.

"Thank you, Marie," Gallad genuinely said, offering her a respectful nod.

"Blackstones, your time is coming to an end," Eloise said, still writing, anchoring the souls of the past to the present, but more comfortably positioned in a nearby recliner.

"Ask about the ornaments before it's too late," Sunny whispered none too quietly from somewhere nearby.

"Right!" Macy blurted. "Will you tell us about the ornaments we hang every year? They're beautiful, and we know some of the history behind them, but coming from you, it would be amazing to know."

They all moved in closer to the ten-foot evergreen in the corner of the room. Decorated and dressed up for the occasion, the tree awaited its moment to light up the holiday.

Judson pointed to a nearby ornament. "This one was my mother's from her family. She settled with the Stronghold witch coven back in Virginia when I was young. And this one," he acknowledged with a warm smile, gliding his hand over iron twisted around a cylindrical piece of wood, "we made for Janella. When the kids were born, we made each of them an ornament."

Cessily hovered around the tree. Her eyes lit up when she saw an extremely fragile hand-painted glass ball. She gestured for Hank to be at her side. Tenderly she kissed his cheek.

"This one was in Cessily's family. She had brought it over from the old country before they immigrated to America," Hank explained.

"It's amazing it made it all the way here without breaking so long ago," Brock said in awe.

"Well, to be honest, when we left Virginia, we had some of the witches traveling with us spell our things to ensure their safe arrival," Marie supplied for an explanation.

"So much history. So many stories," Macy said wistfully.

"It's all yours, but don't dwell on it too long and forget to create your own," Marie strongly encouraged.

"What about the topper?" Eva asked.

"Ah, yes, the topper is my most favorite one." Marie clasped her hands together in excitement. "Isn't it brilliant? One of Judson's amazing creations. He had the idea to create something that could tie us all together, from the past and into the future. You explain it, Jud." Marie playfully elbowed him, prodding him to share the story.

He pretended to have the air knocked out of his stomach, then laughed. "All right. I'm not sure it's as brilliant as she makes it sound. But anyway, I was a blacksmith, as you know, but we also had a friend here at that time who could make amazing things out of wood, like jewelry boxes with hidden drawers and truly anything with gears and sprockets."

"Gregory and Charlotte Trent, right?" Macy asked with excitement, knowing part of the story.

"That's right." Judson nodded. "Anyway, he helped me design and build an ornament to attach at the top of the tree. We buried at the heart of it a small amount of aether from the falls. The magic of the falls—which was magic of neither witch nor hunter—would connect the topper to all future family ornaments by instilling a tiny slice of the same aether within each ornament we wished to bind."

"Unbelievable!" Sunny clapped, her smile almost capable of lighting the room on her own.

"When the topper is clicked into the base, it ignites the aether, thus igniting each additional ornament tied to it," Marie added in a rush.

"It's almost midnight," Aunt Letti shouted.

Uncle Tranner added, "If we're going to do this, we need to do it now."

"Hurry!" the kids all shouted.

"Brock will be placing the tree topper this year. Go ahead and lock it into place, Brock." Lilith nodded to him with a smile.

Brock inhaled through his nose, pulled the topper out of its protective box, then clicked a mechanism at the base of the tree topper ornament. They all heard a click and then a whirring of some interior cogs and gizmos. A pregnant pause filled with anticipation weighed heavily in the room until they saw it.

A flash of blue light erupted in the room, then quickly receded. In descending order, the heirloom ornaments each began to glow one by one until they made their way down the tree in a wrap. The glow wasn't bright, but it gave an extra something magical to the tree.

The collective gasped. Then silence permeated the room. Smiles were bright, and tears gracefully fell from their eyes. The moment was complete.

"I don't know if we will ever be able to do this again, but Marie is right. This ornament, it ties us together: the past, this present, and our future." Macy looked around the room, then her gaze landed on Gallad—her future. "In this moment, we have been reunited with all who we hold dear and all who are a part of us in a variety of ways. Merry Christmas, everyone!" Macy exclaimed.

"Merry Christmas!" everyone returned with a cheer.

The clock struck midnight, and the apparitions of the past quickly said their goodbyes as they faded back into eternal rest. Eloise put down her pen and rested.

"That was amazing!" Sunny said, bouncing over to Brice and grabbing his arm, spinning him around while giggling.

Macy reached out and grabbed Hollis's arm, swinging her around, too. Laughter erupted from everyone including Grandma Eva. They danced merrily around the room, enjoying each other's company. It could have been a moment of sadness at the loss of their loved ones once again, but instead they rejoiced in the moment they had and the memory of having been reunited.

Merry Christmas from the Blackstone family!

Have you read all of the Blackstone Witch Hunters stories by Morgan Wylie?
Reawakened
Dawn of the Witch Hunters
Redefined
Rise of the Witch Hunters
Rediscovered

LUCKY AT LOVE

BY E.J. FECHENDA

A Parker Witch Family Short Story

*M*y jaw practically cracked, the yawn was so big. The day was drawing to a close, and I had just received a last-minute job placement opportunity from Tase Roca, the owner of Mount Mae Ski Resort. One of their human ski instructors had taken a nasty spill on the slopes and broke a leg. With the holidays right around the corner, it was a bad time of year for the resort to be down an employee. I yawned again and contemplated running down the street to grab a coffee at Broastful Brew.

Coffee Haven had already closed for the day. I knew because Harlow, my best friend since we were kids, waved at me through the window when she walked by after her shift. Her boyfriend, Ryker, was with her, and he carried a shopping bag from Callie's Consignments. Ryker was a lion shifter and member of SIN, the Swords of Infernal Night Motorcycle Club, and there was something endearing about seeing the biker, wearing his full leathers, toting around his girlfriend's purchases.

Harlow literally glowed with love these days, and I sighed, the ache of loneliness returning full force. Usually I was pretty good at suppressing it—until I saw one of my friends with their happily-ever-after. I wasn't jealous; it's just that Havenwood Falls was a small town and didn't have a huge gay community, so my prospects were slim. My last serious relationship ended disastrously over two years ago. When I came out to my ex-boyfriend as a witch, he didn't handle it well. You'd think being Black and gay, he would have been more open-minded. Nope. He left—not just me, but Havenwood Falls. I knew the wards that protected the town would have erased his memories within a fortnight.

The holidays were especially hard. Last year, I didn't have a plus-one for the Cold Moon Ball and other parties. I didn't have anyone for this year's ball either, or for the wedding event of the year that was happening Christmas Eve. It could have been worse, though.

Harlow's grandmother and my grandmother were good friends, and a couple of years ago had tried to force an arranged marriage upon Harlow and me. Now that would have been an epic disaster! Fortunately, it never happened, and now my grandmother was too busy teaching potions at the new college campus of the Sun & Moon Academy, so she didn't have time to meddle with my love life.

With a sigh, I hit Enter to save the position entry in the database and cast the spell that was part manifestation and part locator. Magic-enhanced job listings had nothing on regular job boards. The spell my grandmother Patty created over seventy-five years ago caused job openings to appear to only the right candidates, wherever they were located. Monte Tayute had figured out how to merge the spell with tech, which made my job so much easier. Tase had requested a supernatural for this position, so he could avoid being short-staffed by another injury.

About an hour later, I shut my computer down and locked up the office. It was flurrying when I stepped outside, and a fine layer of fresh snow covered everything, but not enough that I had to scrape the windows on my Tahoe. I stopped to pick up a pizza at Napoli's before heading home to my townhome in Havenstone, which was a development right on the edge of town. It was dark when I opened the front door, and with the flick of my wrist and a whispered command, the lights turned on. My cat, Salem, was curled up on the sofa in the living room, and he briefly raised his head to blink at me sleepily and acknowledge my presence, before going back to his nap.

"Lazy familiar," I chided as I toed my boots off. He flicked his tail in response. At least he was a companion, and I wasn't coming home to an empty house. It was too quiet, though. With another command, I turned on the TV and listened to the evening news report in the background as I set the pizza on the counter and wandered upstairs to my bedroom to change.

The night was spent binging pizza and *Lucifer*, who was hot but reminded me of Roman Bishop in a way, which I found mildly disturbing because I was definitely not attracted to that arrogant mage.

I was doing paperwork the next afternoon, after sending my admin home early, when I heard the front door open. While I had my own office, the wall facing the reception area was made of glass, enabling me to see who was coming and going. This was a new design since we had to rebuild the office after the bank next door caught fire last May during an attack on our town. Our businesses shared a wall, so we experienced damage too. A gorgeous man I'd never seen before stood in front of my admin's desk. He was wearing a royal-blue ski jacket that stopped right at his lean hips. His russet hair was windblown, and a smattering of stubble lined his jaw. He looked up from the desk, and our eyes met. His were a deep blue, almost the same color as his coat. When I realized I was staring just a tad too long to be professional, I cleared my throat and stood up to walk out and greet the stranger.

"Curtis Parker," I said, introducing myself and extending my hand for a shake.

"Seamus Day." He shook my hand, and a slight tingle traveled up my arm. Magic ran in this guy's veins, and my magic picked up on it. I wanted to hold onto his hand longer, but I let go, and he shook his arm. "I've found static is always worse during the winter."

I couldn't tell if he was using static as an excuse for the magic exchange between us or if he had no idea and legit thought it was an electric charge. "Nice to meet you, Seamus. How can I help you?"

"I'm here about the ski instructor position. Received the job alert this morning when I was in Grand Junction and thought I'd head directly here. Is the position still available?"

Up close, Seamus had the windburned skin of a skier, with faint tan lines in the outline of goggles around his eyes.

"Yes, it is. Come in and have a seat." I stepped back and gestured to my office. Seamus moved past me, and I caught a whiff of his scent. He smelled clean, like the air after a fresh snow, with a hint of cedar, and it was very appealing. "So tell me about yourself," I prompted, taking my seat across from him.

"Sure. Oh, before I forget." Seamus sat up straighter and unzipped his jacket, revealing a forest green button-down shirt. The top buttons were undone, and I caught a glimpse of the tip of a tattoo on the side of his neck. I wanted to peel the material away and see more. What stories did his body art tell? Seamus pulled papers out from the inside of his jacket and placed them on my desk. "My résumé and references."

I picked up his résumé and gave it a cursory scan. He was from Vermont and had been most recently employed at Killington, where he had been a ski instructor during the winter and helped with maintenance and operating the lifts in the off-season.

"Why leave after three years?"

Seamus smiled and leaned forward, his elbows on the arms of the chair. "It's hard to explain. I love Vermont and loved my job, but I wasn't content. I wasn't where I needed to be and felt drawn to Colorado. Does that make sense?"

"Yes, it does." I returned his smile. His story wasn't unusual. The majority of the supes who weren't born in Havenwood Falls often felt pulled here, like our town was a magical beacon for the supernatural.

"Plus, I've never skied the Rockies. My god, these mountains are majestic."

"That they are," I agreed. "Our box canyon here is pretty special."

Seamus had no idea how special. I wondered if he was open about his magical nature. It wasn't something that was brought up in normal conversation, but it would have to be broached eventually. If Seamus had any plans of residing here, he'd have to be vetted by the Court of the Sun & the Moon, the governing board of Havenwood Falls' supernatural community. There were strict rules to follow to ensure our privacy and safety. Only a few of the town's human residents knew supes lived among them.

I hope he decides to stay. The thought floated through my mind, followed by a wave of emotions—excitement, anticipation . . . desire. I cleared my throat and looked at the résumé again, giving myself a mental slap to focus on business.

"You have a degree in Sustainability from the University of New Hampshire. Tell me about that."

"Climate change is real, and I've seen the devastating impact firsthand when the winters are too warm to create good powder. I have an affinity for nature and lessening our footprint on the planet." Most supernaturals had a deep connection to nature—it was instinct for us to preserve and protect our environment. "I helped implement sustainable practices at Killington." He filled me in on his accomplishments. His blue eyes lit up as he spoke, and I found his enthusiasm for the topic mesmerizing. He was a passionate man, and fuck me, if that didn't make him that much hotter.

"You're way overqualified for this job," I said with a laugh. "You know that right?"

Seamus grinned and shrugged his broad shoulders. "Yeah, I know. But when I read the job alert, I can't explain it—it was like a stirring in my soul, an internal nudge that I was meant to follow through. That sounds bizarre, I know, but it's the truth."

My goddess, the way this man was unabashedly deep and spiritual left me stunned.

"You know what else is bizarre?" Seamus asked, running a hand through his hair. He shook his head and snorted. "Nah, I'll probably blow the interview if I tell you this. You'll think I'm nuts."

"No, I won't." I was a little too quick to correct him in my eagerness to learn everything about him.

He hesitated and leaned back in his chair. Now it was his turn to study me. I could see the indecision written on his face. What did he see? We were about the same age. I was twenty-six, and he graduated high school in 2013, the same year as me. While I was lean and in shape, I wasn't a mountain of muscle like Ryker, but held my own in the looks department with clean-cut dark brown hair and eyes my mom said reminded her of whiskey sitting in sunlight. I was wearing black jeans and boots with a dark gray cable knit sweater. Not a suit, but not slovenly either. Slowly, he nodded as if coming to the conclusion that I was trustworthy. Knowing I had already begun to earn his trust caused something inside of me to awaken.

Leaning forward again, Seamus started to talk. "I was about fifty miles from here when my GPS cut out, but I kept driving. Then the road split. This area is new to me, and I didn't know whether to go right or left. Mine was the only car on the road, and had been for miles, so I came to a complete stop—I was literally at the proverbial fork in the road."

By now I was leaning forward, completely engrossed in his story and the sound of his voice, which was deep and melodic.

"So there I was, lost in contemplation about which direction to choose when suddenly a horn blared, causing me to practically jump out of my skin. I look in the rear-view mirror, and there's a tour bus behind me. Like, it appeared out of nowhere. I quickly pulled over to let the bus pass, and the driver waved at me. This is the wild part. When the bus drove past, I read the writing on the side: *Havenwood Falls* in huge letters. It was like a sign from the universe. The bus went left, and I followed it all the way to town."

"Wow! What luck," I said, even though I knew this had happened before. You didn't find Havenwood Falls; the town had a way of finding you, if you were meant to be here.

"There's more. At one point while I was following the bus, I drove through something. At first, I thought the pressure change in my ears had to do with the elevation, but at that same time, every hair on my body stood on end, like I had an electrical charge. Is there a vortex around here?"

"Something like that," I replied. Seamus had passed through the protective wards my coven, the Luna Coven, established and maintained—a magical barrier to protect the town—and whatever Seamus was, he had reacted to the magic.

"As soon as I passed the *Welcome to Havenwood Falls* sign, it wasn't like déjà vu or something, but a sense of rightness—of being where I needed to be. Whatever journey I had been on had come to an end. That sensation only grew when I walked through your front door. Yes, I am overqualified for the job, but I'm going to listen to my gut and apply for it all the same."

Straight forward and knew what he wanted. I liked that take-charge attitude, and it made him all the more attractive. Whoever Seamus was, he had managed to win me over in less than an hour.

"As far as I'm concerned, it's yours. I just have to do my due diligence and check your references. Do you have somewhere to stay tonight?" It was after six on the East Coast, so I'd have to make calls in the morning.

"Well, I was going to sleep in my car to save money, but I won $500 on a scratch ticket I bought in Grand Junction, so I can spring for a room. Is there a hotel or bed and breakfast in town?"

I was picking up on a pattern in Seamus's life: he had an extraordinary amount of luck. I mentioned this, which caused Seamus to laugh.

"Yeah, my mom calls me Lucky Day. She claims that from the day she found out she was pregnant with me, I was a good-luck charm."

Could Seamus be a leprechaun? Did he know he had magic running through his veins? The more we spoke, I was getting the impression he had no idea. I filed that thought away in my brain as I picked up my office phone and dialed Whisper Falls Inn. I didn't have high hopes that they'd have a vacancy, though. Not during peak season.

The owner, Michaela Petran, answered on the third ring. "Whispers Falls Inn, how may I help you?"

"Michaela, it's Curtis. Listen, I have someone in my office who is new to town and needs a place to stay for a night or two. Do you have any openings?"

"You're in luck. Ordinarily we wouldn't, but I just got a cancellation, not even five minutes ago." Of course, she did. Seamus's lucky streak continued. "Who is this for?"

"I'll bring him over and make the introductions. He's definitely someone you should meet."

I heard movement on the other end and a door close in the background.

"Is he supernatural?" she asked in a hushed tone.

"Yes."

"Do you know what species?"

"No. We'll be over in a few minutes."

Michaela was the newest member of the Court, and I had done my part of alerting her to the fact that there was someone new in town. She would take it from there and start the vetting process. I hung up the phone.

"You're all set," I said to Seamus and stood. "Come on, I'll walk you over. It's just down the street."

"Don't you have work?" Seamus asked, rising from his chair. We were almost the same height; I was about an inch taller, which put him around six feet.

"Perks of being the boss," I said and held up my keys. "Plus, it's quiet this time of year. All of the holiday hiring is done, and I finished payroll this morning." Besides being an employment placement service, Parker's Perfect Placement Agency, or PPP Agency, handled payroll and served as a human resources consultancy for smaller businesses.

I grabbed my wool coat from the rack in the back corner of my office. It was near the heating vent and putting it on was like wrapping myself in a blanket fresh out of the dryer.

I shut lights off as we made our way to the front door. Seamus left ahead of me and waited for me on the sidewalk as I locked up.

"Is it okay to leave my car parked here? I won't get a ticket, will I?" Seamus pointed at an older Volvo wagon that was backed into a parking space in front of the building. The car had more rust than paint.

"You drove that from Vermont?" I asked with amazement, taking in the duct tape holding the bumper in place, and also taking note of the pride sticker in the rear window. My heart rate increased.

"Old Blue never lets me down. She has over 250,000 miles, and the engine still purrs like a kitten."

I assured him he wouldn't get ticketed, and as we made our way down Eleventh Street toward the inn, I pointed out the businesses that lined the street. We passed Into the Mystic New Age Books and Gifts, and when we walked by Sanguine Elixirs, I explained that while the liquor store sold wine from Stone Falls Winery, it wasn't owned by the local vineyard, unlike Soothing Sips, the winery's tasting room located next door. It was late afternoon, and the sun was beginning to dip behind Miles Mountain, painting the clear sky a mural of pinks and oranges, which reflected off of the snow-covered peaks that surrounded the town. As the sun retreated and twilight began to settle in, the old-fashioned lamps that lined the sidewalks and illuminated the paths in the town square blinked on. Each lamp was decorated with greenery and enormous red bows. Most of the storefronts were decorated for the holidays, with garlands strung across the fronts and white or colored lights that added to the festiveness.

Whisper Falls Inn was located right off the southeast corner of the town square. The Petran family had built the Victorian mansion and made it into an inn. It's been in the family ever since. Michaela had taken over management a little over three years ago and had been leaving her mark, including a recent renovation that updated the historic building, bringing it up to code and into the twenty-first century. Salt crunched under our feet as we climbed the front steps that led to the wrap-a-round porch and the front door. Fresh garland and white lights curled around the railings and bannisters. Warm air rushed to greet us when I opened the door. Michaela was behind the front desk and looked up when we came in. Her green-gray eyes, a color unique to her kind, assessed Seamus, already beginning to take measure of him.

I made the introductions. "Michaela's fiancé's brother is the owner of the ski resort. Michaela, Seamus is the new ski instructor. Well, as soon as I contact his references."

"Really? Well, nice to meet you, Seamus. How long will you need a room for?" she asked while typing something on her computer. "If you plan to be here through Christmas, the dining room will be closed for a wedding on Christmas Eve."

"Not just a wedding, but Michaela's getting married," I added.

"Congratulations!" Seamus reached into his right back pocket and pulled out his wallet. "I'll be here just a couple of nights, so that won't be a problem. Finding a place more permanent in town is my next step."

"Do you plan on staying in Havenwood Falls?"

"Yes. I like what I see so far."

I noticed Seamus didn't go into the detail he did with me about being drawn here and the connection he felt. Knowing he opened up to me warmed me from the inside out. I stepped back and let them finish the check-in process.

"The dining room will start serving dinner in half an hour, if you're hungry," Michaela said when she handed the key over.

"He's quite the snack." An older woman's voice said in my ear, and I turned to see Madame Luiza standing next to me.

"Excuse me?" Seamus turned around, and his eyes widened slightly when he took in the grandmotherly figure openly checking him out. His cheeks flushed, which made him all the more adorable. "Err, thank you?"

I glanced over at Michaela, and her eyebrows were raised, making her green-gray eyes even more noticeable.

"You can see her?" she asked.

Seamus turned back to face her. "Yes, is she a guest here?"

Michaela smiled, and her white teeth gleamed in the light. "Something like that. Mammie, go find someone your age to flirt with."

Madame Luiza giggled and glided forward, pinching Seamus's ass before disappearing into thin air. Seamus's mouth dropped open.

"Is she . . . was that?" he stammered.

"Yes. That's the ghost of my aunt Luiza who used to run this place. She's harmless."

So Seamus could see spirits. Interesting. I became even more intrigued about this mystery man from Vermont.

"I got it from here, Curtis," Michaela said as she started to lead Seamus up the wide staircase to the bedrooms. The vetting process had begun. I had to step back and let the Court do its thing. I worried that Seamus wasn't prepared for the curveball he was about ready to be served. I said goodnight and promised Seamus I'd be in touch as soon as I did my due diligence with his background check.

That night *Lucifer* failed to hold my interest. My thoughts were consumed by another man. I flicked off the TV and grabbed my laptop. It took a few attempts to get connected to the Wi-Fi—Havenwood Falls was like a black hole for tech sometimes—but I finally managed to search Seamus. His social media presence was light, but from what I found, he was who he said he was. Most of the images were of him skiing or partying. One picture of him embracing a blond man caused my stomach to tighten. He hadn't mentioned being in a relationship.

Whoa, I scolded myself and snapped the laptop shut, startling Salem who had curled up next to me. He gave me the side-eye and slunk off the sofa. Yeah, I was crossing the line and needed to maintain a level of professionalism. Turning the television back on, I channel surfed until coming across *A Christmas Story*. I watched it for a while and wound up falling asleep.

The following morning was spent reaching out to Seamus's references. Every single one raved about him and said if I didn't hire him, to send him back because they would. It was probably the easiest background check I'd ever done. Of course, it went smoothly. That was Seamus's luck, right? I chuckled over the charmed life he must lead. I called Tase with the good news.

"Want to hire him?" I asked after relaying all of Seamus's information.

"Fuck, yes. Can he start today? We're slammed since the Halvard campus started winter break."

"I'll bring him up this afternoon."

Less than twenty minutes after contacting Seamus to offer him the position, he was walking through the door with a cup of coffee in his hand. I recognized the Coffee Haven logo. He was wearing black jeans and a black turtleneck underneath the same blue jacket he had on the day before. I observed his confident swagger as he walked toward me.

"Man, this is some good java," he said and dropped down in his chair in front of my desk.

His clean scent washed over me, and I couldn't help but breathe deep, hoping he didn't notice. I liked how he walked in like he had already made himself at home here.

"I'm telling you, Curtis, today is my lucky day." He winked at me and took a sip from his cup. "A new job and I mentioned to the owner of Coffee Haven, Willow, I think her name is? Anyway, I mentioned that I was new to town, and she offered to rent me the apartment upstairs from her shop."

Willow was a Seelie fae and a powerful empath. She must have picked up on some good vibes from Seamus to offer her apartment to him right off the bat. That was a good sign.

"That's great!"

Seamus was staying. This gave me time . . . us time. *Us?* I was getting ahead of myself and had to look away from his blue eyes. Swiveling in my chair, I grabbed the stack of new hire paperwork off of the filing cabinet that was against the wall behind my desk. While Seamus filled out forms, I went to make copies of his identification and social security card.

After getting the paperwork in order, we headed over to the resort. Seamus followed me, and even though the drive was short, I occasionally looked in my rear-view mirror to make sure Old Blue hadn't broken down, but the rusty Volvo handled the turns and icy roads just fine.

The lifts were at capacity, and skiers dotted the slopes, their jackets a bright array of colors. We walked into the lodge and over to the front desk where an employee radioed Tase. Moments later, I spotted the tall moroi vampire moving through the crowded lobby from the back. People seemed to move subconsciously out of his way. When he reached us, I made the introductions and handed Tase the paperwork. My job here was done, which meant I was free to pursue Seamus, and I planned to.

"Thanks, Parker. Your services are worth every penny," Tase said and shook my hand. "Send me the invoice."

"I will." I turned to Seamus. "Call if you need anything, okay?" I handed him my card.

"Definitely. Thanks for everything, man."

I watched as he and Tase walked toward the main entrance, which led out to the slopes. I noticed Michaela waiting by the doors with Elsmed Fairchild. The elder Court member looked out of place among the skiers. The fae was wearing a wool dress coat over a three-piece suit, and his long silver hair blew whenever the door opened. Seamus's new hire orientation was going to be boring compared to his new resident orientation. *Go easy on him*, I thought in my head. Elsmed met my eyes from across the room and nodded. Of course, he read my mind. At least my message was received. I'd hate for Seamus to find out the truth about Havenwood Falls and run away screaming. The idea of him leaving made my stomach ache. He only just got here.

My worst fear came true when less than two hours later, Seamus burst through the front door of my office. His face was pale except for splotches of red high on his cheekbones. My assistant jumped up to stop him, but he moved too fast. As soon as he was in my office, he shut the door and sat down. He was breathing heavy and clearly agitated. My assistant stared at me through the glass window, and I waved at her to let her know I was okay. She pursed her lips and shook her head before turning around to sit at her desk again.

"Seamus, what's going on?" I asked in a soothing tone.

"They're fucking crazy. Unless this is a joke? Am I being punked or something? This Court or whatever claims I'm a leprechaun. A fucking leprechaun!" He let out a high-pitched laugh.

Fuck. The orientation with the Court hadn't gone well. Just as I suspected, Seamus didn't know about his supernatural DNA. I didn't say anything, but my expression must have.

"You knew?" he spit out, and my heart ached. He thought I betrayed his trust.

"It's true, Seamus. What they told you. It's all true." To prove to him, I snapped my fingers, and the blinds on the window rolled down, giving us privacy.

He jumped at the sound and turned to see them roll down on their own.

"What are you?" He faced me with narrowed eyes.

I sighed and pinched the bridge of my nose. "I'm a witch and member of the Luna Coven."

"A witch?" He stared at me as if trying to see something

different under my skin, like I was wearing a mask. Unlike some supernaturals, I didn't have to use a glamour to disguise my true features. I looked as human as the next guy.

"The fact that you received that job alert wasn't an accident. You responded to the call." I explained to him the process of using spell-casting to attract the right job candidates. The more I talked, the more he calmed down. He was listening and processing. He hadn't run away . . . yet.

"Come on. You look like you could use a drink. I'll buy you a beer or three, and I'll answer any questions. Okay?"

He nodded and stood. "You're really a witch?"

In response, I snapped my fingers, and my coat lifted off the rack, then floated through the air and into my waiting hand.

"Holy shit!" His eyes were so wide, the whites overwhelmed the blue. "That's . . . that's, um, actually kind of cool."

I thought about taking him to Soothing Sips, but the conversation we were about to have required a bar, so we walked halfway around the block to Haven Saloon. It was still fairly early, so not very crowded. A few people sat at the long, gleaming wooden bar where Brent was mixing a martini. The skunky odor of marijuana hung in the air. I guided us to a table in the corner, away from everyone else. Brent came over to take our orders, and he recommended Mountain Top Ale, a holiday ale Blackstone Brothers Micro Brews was testing out. We went with his suggestion, and Brent returned minutes later with two pint glasses filled to the brim. Once he left us alone, I cast a muffling spell around the table so no one could hear us talk.

After taking a few sips, I unbuttoned my dress shirt sleeves and rolled them up, revealing my tattoo on my inner arm. It was a series of the moon in its phases: waxing, full, and waning. The full moon was filled in with rainbow colors as a representation of gay pride. Seamus set his glass down and reached for my arm, pulling it toward him across the table. His finger traced my tattoo, sending zings of sensation up my arm and back down again, as my magic reached up to meet his.

"Do you feel that?" I asked in a soft voice even though no one could hear us.

"The static?" He looked up at me, his eyes locking on mine.

"That's not static. My magic is responding to yours."

His hand holding my arm shook briefly, and I noticed he swallowed hard. Licking his lips, he glanced back down at my tattoo and continued to trace. I stayed still and let him get used to the sensation. His touch was sweet torture and making me aroused.

"I never knew who my dad was," he said suddenly, releasing my arm and breaking the sexual tension. "My mom said I was the result of a one-night stand, but she kept me, raised me, and loved me. That was enough. I never had any urge to find him." He reached for his glass and drained half of it in one gulp. "Apparently, my father was a leprechaun." He snorted and shook his head in disbelief. "A fucking leprechaun. I'm not short or green, and where the hell is my pot of gold?"

"Well, you did win the lottery yesterday," I said, referencing his scratch ticket winnings. "And while Leprechauns are wee folk, clearly your human genes are dominant."

"Not exactly a pot of gold, but I guess my being lucky isn't just coincidence. Huh." He seemed to relax then, his shoulders dropped and he leaned back in his seat.

Thank the goddess; he was coming to terms with the bomb that had just dropped on him. "The Court told you about the rules and what happens with your memory if you decide not to stay, right? This could all be wiped clean like it never happened."

He nodded and took another sip. "I'm not going to lie and say everything is great, because I'm a little freaked."

I couldn't imagine. I've always known I was a witch. My ancestors escaped Salem, Massachusetts, narrowly avoiding being executed. As soon as I could walk, my parents were teaching me the craft.

Our glasses were empty, and I gestured to Brent for refills. He brought them over, and I introduced him to Seamus.

"Is he something?" Seamus asked after Brent walked away.

"No, he's human. But that woman over there—" I gestured to Jetta Mills, who was setting up a microphone and amplifier. Her guitar case was propped against the wall.

"Yeah?"

"She's a frost dragon."

"A what?"

"She shifts into a dragon."

"Jesus fucking Christ, my mind is blown." His elbows were on the table, and he was cradling his head, his long fingers buried in his hair. I hated seeing him distressed like this. All the confidence he had on display earlier was gone. It was like a wrecking ball had smashed it apart.

"Hey." I reached across the table and grabbed one of his hands, rescuing his hair from its clutches. His skin was rough and warm, his magic rising to meet mine again. "It's a lot to take in, but you are meant to be here. If you stay, I'll help you adjust, and the other supes will, too."

"Yeah." Seamus leaned back, breaking our contact. "I have a lot to think about." He chewed on his bottom lip, while staring at his pint glass, which was almost empty. I lost track of how many rounds we'd had. All I knew was that between his magic and the beer, my head was swimming. I could tell Seamus was drifting, getting lost in his thoughts, and I knew he needed to be alone to figure things out.

"Hey, what's your number?" I asked him while grabbing my cell phone from my back pocket. He rattled it off, and I saved him as a contact, then immediately sent him a text. "There, now you have my cell. Call me anytime. I'm sure you'll have more questions."

We stood up, and I nodded at Brent, silent acknowledgment that I would settle up with him later. I watched as Seamus put on his coat. It caused his shirt to rise, revealing serious abdominals. My gaze traveled up to his chest and broad shoulders, and when I finally met his eyes, I realized he was watching me, too. He winked at me and gave me a wicked grin, which made my mouth go dry.

I wasn't in any condition to drive, and Seamus wasn't either. We walked down Main Street toward the inn. Our arms brushed against each other as we drew closer, and each contact made my pulse thrum. Although it was dark, it was still early, and the sidewalks were busy with diners and shoppers, but we were in our own bubble. When we reached the corner, we paused out front of Simple Treasures Pawn Shop.

"Thank you, Curtis," Seamus said. He placed his hand on my shoulder and gave it a light squeeze before trailing his fingers down the length of my arm. He stood in a halo of light from the streetlamp on the corner. His cheeks were flushed, his eyes glassy and bright, and his hair moved in the light wind. That image would be forever burned in my mind. In that golden glow, everything otherworldly about him seemed to be revealed. He couldn't pass as human; even his skin seemed to shine. He was absolutely the most gorgeous man I'd ever laid eyes on.

"Good night, Seamus. I like you and hope you decide to stay." Emboldened by the fact that he might choose to leave and I'd never see him again, I stepped forward, closing the gap between us. My eyes lowered to his lips, telegraphing my intent, and Seamus tilted his head slightly, giving me his answer. I curled my hand around the back of his neck, and he pressed against me, his arms slinking around my waist, as my mouth slanted over his. He tasted of beer and mint Chapstick, a surprisingly delicious combination. He groaned when my tongue slipped past his parted lips. My heart was pounding, and blood rushed through my body, making my arousal obvious. When he moved his hips, pressing closer to me, I could tell he was having the same reaction.

A car drove by, and someone, probably a high school kid, whooped out the open window at us, breaking up the moment. Seamus started to laugh, and I soon followed, effectively ending one fucking amazing kiss.

"Well, good night . . . again," I said with a smile. "This is a great town. I think you'll be happy here."

Seamus nodded and looked around the square and all the storefronts lit up. "Yeah, there is a lot for me to consider." He winked, shoved his hands in his pockets, and turned, stepping toward the curb. "Good night, Curtis."

With that, he crossed the street. I watched him walk away. The ache I felt at his departure surprised me. We had barely met, only shared one very public kiss that had been the most intimate kiss of my life, but I wanted so much more—with him and only him.

I debated calling a Luber, but decided to walk home. Flurries drifted down and swirled in the occasional gust of wind. The tiny crystals melted fast once they landed on my flushed cheeks. I got home and quickly changed, heating up a pot pie for dinner, which Salem gladly shared. After eating, nothing held my attention. My thoughts were with Seamus and whether he would decide to stay.

Hopefully our kiss gave him something more to think about. *Please don't let these feelings be one sided*, I whispered into the universe.

I snatched my cell phone off the coffee table and texted Harlow.

Me: How did you know Ryker was the one?

Harlow: You just know

Harlow: Wait, that's a lame answer. I would die for him and I thought I was whole until he filled a part of me I didn't know was missing

Me: That sounds like some you complete me Jerry Maguire bullshit

Harlow: Well, there's truth to it. When I imagine my life without him, I get bereft at the very thought

Me: Like an ache?

Harlow: Yeah, exactly. Why are you asking? Did you meet someone?

Me: I think so

Harlow: CURTIS PARKER I NEED DETAILS!

Me: Are you at CH tomorrow?

Harlow: YES

Me: I'll stop by and fill you in then

Harlow: YOU BETTER!

I laughed at her use of all caps and pictured her with her hands on her hips, giving me the stare down.

Sleep came in bits and pieces, so by the time the sun started to peek through my blinds an hour before my alarm was supposed to go off, I gave up and got out of bed. I changed into my running gear, pulled on a fleece, and headed out for a run to burn off nervous energy. I ran up toward the falls and looped around the cemetery before running through the square, a short cut to Coffee Haven. The bell above the door chimed when I opened it and stepped into sweet scented warmth, breathing in the aroma of fresh brewed coffee and baked goods.

Harlow was behind the long counter, steaming milk for a latte, but she looked up when she heard the bell.

"Parker! Get your ass over here," she said with a grin. I started to walk toward her, the wooden floorboards creaking under my feet, when I saw Seamus sitting at a table by himself. He had already noticed me, and he smiled.

"Can I talk to you?" he asked.

Coffee and Harlow forgotten, I sat across from him. He reached for my hand, and I welcomed his touch. His eyes were bloodshot and heavy, making me think he barely slept at all, too.

"I was going to call you later, but I'm glad you're here so I can tell you in person."

Had he decided to leave? The thought of not seeing him again formed a lump in my throat along with a pit in my stomach.

"I almost left yesterday. After that crazy ass meeting, I got in my car and started to leave, but then you popped into my head, so I drove to your office instead. I don't know why, but I just knew you would hear me out and help me make sense of things." He paused, and I squeezed his hand, encouraging him to continue. "While I still don't one-hundred-percent understand, I know I can't run from this. I know the cost of hiding my identity. I didn't come out to my mom until my senior year of high school, although she said she always knew." He smiled and stared out the window, lost in the memory. I admired his profile, his straight nose and sharp jawline. He turned his attention back to me. "I refuse to pretend I'm someone else. I need to live my truth, and if my truth is that I'm part—" he leaned forward and whispered, "*leprechaun*, then Havenwood Falls is the place where I can be myself and where I won't be alone." This time he squeezed my hand, causing my magic to rise to meet his.

"So you're staying?" My eyes locked on his, and he nodded.

"Your kiss last night was pretty persuasive, too. I think you made up my mind then." He licked his lips as if tasting us. Us. Oh, how I wanted there to be an *us*.

"Well, I can think of a great way to get to know your new home and to help assimilate," I said, and Seamus raised an eyebrow, curiosity piqued. "How do you feel about going to Michaela and Xandru's wedding with me?"

Meet Curtis in Harlow and Ryker's story, *Stray With Me*, a Sin & Silk novella.

FOREVER LOVE

BY SUSAN BURDORF

A Rusty & Sherry Short Story

S herry stepped from the shower. As she reached for a towel, she was pulled back into the steam, forcing a squeal of surprise and then a giggle as she was wrapped in the strong, insistent arms of her husband of almost one year. Rusty crushed her against his chest, pressing his lips to hers as his tongue found her open mouth, and kissed her long and deep.

Sighing with pleasure, Sherry returned the kiss with a hunger of her own. The pulse of warm water turned tepid then cold as they explored each other's bodies as if they hadn't made love in the comfort of their bed just a short time before.

"I have to go," Sherry said. Her voice was breathless as she reluctantly pushed her husband backward. "I'm meeting Ruby and Cece for some last-minute shopping after coffee and scones in about an hour."

"Great," Rusty said pulling her back into his embrace. "Plenty of time to . . ." His words were lost as he nuzzled her neck. Shivers of delight tingled down her spine where his hands traveled to the small of her back. He gripped one wet buttock before pressing her tightly against his firm body as if pulling her inside himself.

"Rusty." Sherry placed both her hands on the side of his face, staring into his soft brown eyes with desire that matched his. "I really have to go."

Sighing, Rusty reached around her to turn off the water. "I just hope they realize what I'm sacrificing for your coffee."

Sherry laughed at Rusty's overly dramatic disappointment and slapped his taut bare buttocks with the towel as they stepped from the shower.

He leaned toward her, his bare torso heating the air around her with his musky scent. "Do that again, wife," he said, his voice deep with promise, "and your coffee and scones will have to wait."

"Oh?" said Sherry with a giggle, towel poised for another strike. "And what will you do to stop me?"

Rusty grinned, his eyes locking onto hers, his arms reaching for her, but Sherry danced back, abandoning her plans to thwack him again as she raced for the bedroom.

He tackled her onto the bed, hugging her to his body, stretching out the length of his hard lines against her softer skin as he kissed her soundly before bouncing off the bed and dressing so fast she barely had time to watch his muscles flex.

"Be careful today, Sherry. There've been reports of some unusual folks in town."

Sherry sat up, concern etching lines between her brows. "Dangerous?"

"No, just . . . odd. Ric has me patrolling a bit more carefully around the forest. This time of year always brings out the pranksters and a few elements we need to watch out for. Just be careful. Keep Ruby and Cece near you at all times and you should be fine."

Sherry nodded. Rusty's cousin, Ric Kasun was sheriff of Havenwood Falls. If the two of them were worried, then she knew he was telling the truth about being careful.

But really, Sherry thought when Rusty had walked out the door, what could happen to her in Havenwood Falls?

As always, Sherry thought, glancing around the square in downtown Havenwood Falls, the town had outdone itself with decorations for the holiday. Wide red ribbons mixed with bright green garlands smelling of the nearby forest were strung around light poles and across the fronts of buildings, giving the whole town the effect of being an alternative to the North Pole. Red, gold, and silver baubles and ornaments played peek-a-boo with the green while both colored and clear white lights sparkled everywhere.

Crowds of tourists from the local ski resort milled about in their bright parkas, adding color to the festive air. Their excited voices as they wandered in and out of the local shops brought a smile to her lips. As an author, she was a people-watcher, and standing outside Coffee Haven while she waited for Ruby and Cece to arrive, Sherry found the merriment and energy of people going about their holiday errands intoxicating.

She just wished she could feel the same joy as the people around her. She was one present short of a perfect holiday. Rusty was the worst one to buy gifts for. She had the usual—socks, a new sweater she'd knitted him in secret, a new pair of boots, and some of his favorite cologne—but she wanted something else and was having a horrible time finding it. Thus, she was meeting with Cece and Ruby to pick their brains for some suggestions.

She'd perused magazine after magazine, scrolled through suggested gifts on her laptop, but hadn't found the one that would tell him just how much she loved him. They'd married at Christmastime one year ago, forgoing gifts to celebrate their love by formalizing their union, but now a year had passed, and so much had happened to the town and to them in that year. She was struggling to find the gift that would tell him just how special she felt he was. He'd reassured her time and time again that just having her in his life was all he needed, but that wasn't enough for her. She had never felt this special, this loved in her entire life, and she wanted to be sure he knew just how much she loved him.

Just thinking about their lovemaking earlier that morning gave her a thrill, and she shivered in the chill air, wishing he was with her now, but he was off on one of his patrols around Havenwood Falls and wouldn't be home for hours yet.

"Hello, Sherry!" Cece and Ruby called and waved at her from across the street.

Sherry waved back, her smile wide and genuine at the sight of her two best friends.

Ruby Howe, the elderly witch who ran Howe's Herbal Shoppe, was the first to greet her with a hug and a smile. "No coffee yet?"

"Nope. I know, big surprise, but I wanted to wait for you two." Sherry shifted her purse to her other hand and gestured toward the entrance as Cece joined them.

Cece squeezed her arm, her eyes locking on Sherry's in concern. "You okay, dear?"

"Oh, yes, I'm fine," Sherry reassured her friend. Sometimes, Cece's ability to read her mind was disconcerting. As an angel, Cece had a talent for knowing when people were sad or worried and was always ready with a comforting look or touch. Sherry kept a wide smile on her face, knowing it didn't quite reach her eyes, hoping Cece wouldn't press her for a reason yet.

"Come on, I need coffee," Sherry said as her friends laughed.

Once they'd placed their order, grabbed their fresh-from-the-oven blueberry scones, and claimed seats vacated by a family of tourists, Sherry sighed.

"Okay, spill. Why did you need to meet us?" Ruby asked, tilting her head as she studied Sherry over the top of the scone she'd raised to her lips.

Sherry cleared her throat. "You know this is Rusty's and my first anniversary, right?"

Both friends nodded.

"We were at the wedding," Cece said drily around a bite of scone.

Sherry chuckled. "Yes, yes, you were. And thanks for that little surprise."

"You're welcome," Cece said, her eyes twinkling with amusement.

"I don't know what to get Rusty for our anniversary. I have just one more gift I want to get him, and it is the most important one. But I can't think of a thing that it could be."

"Ah . . ." Cece and Ruby looked at each other then back at Sherry.

"What do you get for a wolf shifter who pretty much has

everything he needs?" Sherry asked, lowering her voice so no one could overhear her as there were a lot of tourists nearby, none of whom would quite understand that she was married to a supernatural. Some of the locals were aware of the fact some people in town were different, but most were also unaware of just how special some people were.

"Did you ask him what he wants?" Ruby said.

"Sure, and he says he has everything he needs."

"Well, then, that's your answer," Cece said.

"No, I have to get something special, something amazing for him. He's so wonderful. I . . . I have never felt so loved, so completely completed. I need to get him something that tells him that. But I can't think of anything." Sherry threw her hands up in the air in frustration.

Both of her friends reached out, and each took one of her hands.

Sherry felt their energy as warmth and calmed almost immediately at their combined touch.

"So," Cece said slowly as she removed her hand, "I understand humans celebrate the first anniversary with paper. Maybe you could get him a new book? You are a writer, after all. Perhaps there is a special book you like that he might enjoy, too?"

"Or write him a letter telling him how much you love him?" Ruby suggested.

"That's good, Ruby," Cece said. Nodding at Ruby, she turned to Sherry. "A letter sounds like a great idea. Maybe use special paper, or a special pen in his favorite color, and write him a letter or a poem expressing how you feel. You are working on that book, still, right? Well, then this would be right up your alley."

Sherry frowned as she considered Ruby's suggestion. "That's not a bad idea."

"Okay, well, I have to go," Cece stood up. Taking her departure as a signal, Ruby and Sherry followed. The table was immediately occupied by one of the groups waiting for a place to sit.

Outside the coffee shop, the three women chatted for a minute before Cece left, leaving Ruby and Sherry to walk down the street checking out the shops for that last elusive gift.

Sherry checked out watches, and wallets, and whimsical toys, but none struck her as something Rusty would like. In the back of her mind, she was thinking about Ruby's suggestion of writing a letter; she just wasn't sure what to say, how to let him know how much he'd changed her life for the better.

"That's odd," Ruby said. She was frowning as she stared into the front window of Callie's Consignments. A few items were displayed as gift ideas. Prominent in the front was a rectangular metal box with a strange symbol on top in gold-flecked paint. A packet of paper edged in gold and a pen with a fancy feather, pure white with golden edges, were displayed with the box.

Sherry couldn't take her eyes from the box that had caught the older woman's attention.

"What's odd?"

Ruby pointed at it. "I don't remember seeing that earlier."

"I love that. I think that would be the perfect paper to write the letter to Rusty with," Sherry said. She couldn't take her eyes from the box.

"It's quite pretty, but—" Ruby turned to Sherry, about to say more, but Sherry was already heading inside the shop. Ruby followed at a slower pace, frown lines creasing her forehead.

Sherry went immediately to the display window and pointed to the box.

"Would you like this, Sherry?" Nikita asked. She was Callie's cousin, helping run the store while Callie had been traveling, searching for new pieces and coming home often enough to keep her memories. Actually, Sherry thought she'd seen Callie back in town for the holidays—and probably the upcoming big wedding—the other day. Sherry didn't know Nikita as well as she did Callie, but she had a darker, more mysterious air about her, coming from Callie's demon side of the family.

"Yes, I would. Thank you!" She smiled with happiness as the box was taken from the window.

Nikita put the pen and paper inside before snapping it closed tightly. "Mustn't let the magic out."

Sherry frowned. "Magic?"

"Oh, yes," she said with a tight smile that didn't quite reach the eyes. "Words are their own kind of magic. A perfect gift can only come from the words that speak from the heart. Wouldn't you agree?"

Before Sherry could react, Nikita reached out and clasped her hand. Sherry shivered at the touch, a small spark of static electricity tingling up her arm, but disappearing almost immediately when their hands separated.

"I do agree," Sherry said, accepting the package after paying for her purchase.

Ruby caught up to her just as Sherry stepped away from the counter. Ruby looked at Nikita, who nodded then turned away. The witch took Sherry's arm and walked out of the store.

"Are you okay, Ruby?" Sherry asked.

"Yes, I am." Ruby looked Sherry in the eyes with such intensity, the younger woman stepped away with a confused expression.

"Are you sure, because you look a little worried," Sherry said.

"Did anything strange happen while you were in there?"

"Strange?" Sherry repeated. She thought for a second before answering her friend. "No, not really."

"Hmm . . ." was all Ruby said.

"I need to get home," Sherry said after the two had walked around the square again. "I am going to write this letter before Rusty comes home. Talk to you later?"

They'd reached Howe's Herbal Shoppe. Sherry watched Ruby head inside before leaving for home—but first, coffee.

Once she arrived home, Sherry dropped her purchases on the table. She couldn't wait to open the box and check out the paper and pen. Her fingers were itching to get started on the letter. In her mind, she was composing the perfect letter to Rusty, describing her feelings and how much she wanted their love to last forever.

Sherry opened the stationery kit with excitement. It was perfect. The paper was as beautiful as she remembered, crisp and satisfying to the touch as only high-quality parchment could be. The pen included in the set fit perfectly in her hand, almost as if made for her. She could feel it warming to her touch. She shook the pen, splattering a little ink on the page. Reaching for a tissue, she went to wipe it off the paper only to discover the spots were gone.

"*Well, that's weird*," Sherry thought. She lifted the page to see if the ink had bled through to the pages beneath, but there was nothing there.

"Hmm . . ." Tapping the pen against her chin, she thought about what she wanted to write.

Dearest Rusty,

When we first met, that fateful night on the road when my car crashed, I never thought I would be rescued by the sexiest man in Havenwood Falls. Living here has taught me that love is not just the words you say, but the way you show it.

Every day you teach me something new about love, and life, and what forever means. This Christmas, our first anniversary, is a reminder of all we have ever been and all we will ever be.

If I could ever wish for anything, it would be for this: I wish for us to have forever. I wish for me to always be right here. Always waiting for you to come home. You are the best present I could ever have wished for. I hope I am the same for you this Christmas.

All My Love,

Sherry

Reading the letter over, Sherry smiled. She sealed the letter with a kiss, pressing her lips to the paper and leaving a faint pink impression of her lipstick. As she laid the pen down, she felt a strange tingling start at her toes. Looking down, she was shocked to see her legs disappearing, then her hips, then her waist, her arms . . . closing her eyes, she let out a sigh whispering, "*Rusty,*" as the rest of her body swirled into nothingness.

The paper lifted upward, glowing with a brilliant shade of blue-white light before settling back onto the table as if a breeze had ruffled the edges before leaving the room.

Rusty walked in the door calling Sherry's name but was met with silence.

The house appeared to be empty but smelled strongly of magic. He stepped into the room carefully, his senses alert. He noticed Sherry's purse on the table near the door. Wrapping paper, tape, ribbons, and boxes, both wrapped and not, lay haphazardly on the floor. On the dining room table, he noticed a bright blue tin box, some paper, and a pen, none of which he'd ever seen before.

The smell of magic was strongest there, but he couldn't tell why. Everything looked normal; nothing looked out of place except that Sherry was nowhere to be seen. Her coat, purse, and boots were in their usual places. A coffee cup sat on the table. He touched it, but it was cold.

Stepping outside to see if perhaps Sherry was there, he was confused to not find her anywhere. Her smell outside was faint, as if she'd not been out there for a long time. He stepped back inside just as his phone buzzed. He grabbed it quickly, thinking Sherry must be calling him. Looking at the caller ID, he was surprised to see Ruby's name.

"Hello, Ruby, what's up?" He opened the bedroom door, only to find it empty, too. The smell of their morning lovemaking hung faintly in the air.

". . . Sherry."

Rusty caught his wife' name and brought his attention back to Ruby. "What was that, Ruby? What did you say about Sherry?"

"I asked if I could talk to her. I've been trying to call her, but she's not picking up her phone."

"Well, I would love to talk to her, too. I just got home, and it looks like she was wrapping gifts, but she's not here. But, Ruby, I smell magic. I smell magic all over the cabin. Nothing seems wrong, except she's not here."

"Oh, dear," Ruby said. Her tone caught Rusty by surprise, and he felt his wolf surging inside. Ruby was taking too long to tell him what happened. Sherry was in danger; he knew it. He just didn't know what kind of danger.

"What's wrong, Ruby? Why'd you say it like that?"

Instead of answering, Ruby hesitated for a few seconds. "Do you see anything like a blue metal stationery box around with a weird symbol on top?"

"Stationery?" Rusty was confused. Why would Ruby want paper?

"Yes, Sherry and I saw an unusual stationery set at Callie's Consignments, and she bought it. I think there might be something wrong with it. I can't explain, but I need to see it. Can I come over?"

Rusty looked over to the table with the box, papers, and pen he'd noticed earlier. Walking over to it, he saw a paper with writing on it resting on top of several blank sheets. The writing was definitely hers.

Reaching for the papers, he hesitated. The overpowering smell of magic filled his nostrils, and he backed away. His growled an internal warning.

"Where are you, Sherry? Why can I feel you, but not see you?" he thought.

"Rusty?"

He could hear Ruby calling him from the phone but couldn't respond. Between fighting to control his wolf and the overwhelming sense that Sherry was right there, right in front of him, his brain fogged, his movements became inexplicably sluggish and difficult. Just opening his mouth to speak took more effort than before, as if he'd walked inside a wall and didn't know the way out, yet the room was clearly before him like always. Walls, table, chairs, even the fire burning at the end of the room was visible and real.

Closing his eyes, he breathed deeply, focusing his energy on the things he could see and touch. Opening his eyes, he reached for the table in front of him, which became an anchor that held him down, brought his consciousness back. The fogging in his mind cleared. The throbbing from the repression of his wolf lessened to a bearable level. The knowledge that something unusual had happened in this room didn't go away, but the need to protect from an unseen danger did recede in his mind. He had no clue what he was facing, but he knew Sherry was at the center of whatever occurred in the room.

He took a deep, shuddering breath. He needed help, and he needed it quickly.

"Ruby, do you need me to pick you up? I definitely think you need to come here."

"Yes, I agree. I will be there as quick as I can. Stay there."

Rusty mumbled his agreement.

He paced the room while he waited, trying to find the source of the power. Although the smell of magic was still strongest around the table, he resisted the urge to touch the paper, didn't even look at it, afraid reading it might create more trouble than he was prepared to handle without knowing what was going on.

He knew enough about Havenwood Falls magic to know that messing with things you didn't understand was a sure-fire way to get yourself into deep shit.

Rusty walked outside and waited for Ruby on the porch. His stomach muscles were tight with the fear pounding in his chest. He paced back and forth on the porch. He could feel his inner wolf begging for freedom, but he controlled the need to release him. What could his wolf do now? Fighting magic like this was not something shifting into his wolf could help him with.

He kept repeating over and over in his mind, *what kind of magic was in his house?*

Where was Sherry?

In about ten minutes, Ruby arrived. She was carrying a small bag.

Ruby nodded to him as she walked past him and into the house.

Following behind, Rusty watched her prepare. Her expression was grim, her posture stiff and purposeful—she was ready for battle.

Ruby strode to the table where the box lay. Carefully moving the paper with her wand, she read the letter. Sighing, Ruby shook her head and muttered a short spell under her breath that momentarily brought the words from the page to burn in the air around her.

The pungent smell of sulfur and a deeper magic spell lingered briefly in the air. Rusty's nose twitched, and he frowned.

Deep lines creased her brow as Ruby considered her next move.

Rusty moved closer. "What's going on, Ruby? What's happened to Sherry?"

"I'm afraid this paper's been spelled to create a trap for whoever uses it."

"What kind of trap?" Rusty was angry, but controlled.

Ruby appreciated his ability to maintain somewhat calm. She was seething with anger inside.

"This paper has been touched with a spell that pulls the writer into their own words. We have to go on a hunt to find her, using her words as the clues."

"So she's still alive, but trapped someplace?"

"Yes." Ruby nodded. "She's near us right now, I think."

Rusty glanced around quickly. "I can't see her."

"No, and you won't because she's here, but not here. She's caught in a dimension between us. The spell the paper is enchanted with is called a wish-spell, and the wish of the writer is used to capture them."

"How do we get her back?"

"We have to follow the clues in her letter."

"Clues?" Rusty looked at the paper on the table and reached for it, stopping when Ruby touched him with her wand on his wrist.

"Don't touch the paper. I believe that if you touch it, you will be caught in another dimension and you'll both be lost forever. This kind of spell has a very short shelf life. But that's not good. Basically, we have until midnight to free her, or she'll be trapped inside forever."

"Huh?" said Rusty. He pulled his hand back, his eyes not leaving the paper.

"There's also a double twist on that spell. If you touch that paper and are drawn into the spell, then you can't save Sherry. Only *you* can break the spell holding her inside her words."

Rusty gulped.

"Now," said Ruby as she opened the bag she'd brought with her, "we get to work. I am going to try a couple of counter-spells I know to see if that will help before we work on the clues she left us."

An hour later, with several spells tried and every one of them failing, Ruby sat back. Glancing at the clock, she noticed the time was edging closer to midnight. Four hours left to defeat the spell.

Through her attempts to break the spell, Rusty had remained nearby, watching and waiting.

"Should we call for help?"

Ruby shook her head. "I know we can do this."

"Why Sherry?"

Ruby hesitated before answering. "I'm not sure. I don't think she was targeted. I think it was just a random act. Not purposeful, unless keeping her trapped gains the spellcaster something, which might be the case. Maybe a demon needing a soul? I'm not sure. All I know is, we have to get her out of there as soon as possible. And I think what happens next will need to come from you."

"What do I need to do?" Rusty moved to stand beside Ruby. He reached out, but stopped just short of actually touching the paper. He read Sherry's words then frowned. "I think we need to follow the clues in her letter now. I think we need me to go where she mentions in the letter. Like the place where we first met. That was on the road not too far from here when I accidentally caused her car to go off the road."

"Yes, I think so, too. Let's go."

When they arrived at the place where Sherry first met Rusty, his wolf sense went haywire, and he immediately felt danger. Standing beside Ruby, he looked into the forest around them, searching for a reason he was on edge.

A shadow separated from the trees and glided toward them. Ruby stiffened, and Rusty squeezed her arm. She relaxed and waited for the shadow to form itself into Nikita's form, although this thing was not Nikita.

Ignoring Ruby, the figure turned toward Rusty. Its lower jaw creased into a smile that chilled his heart. He knew immediately there would be no help given by this creature, but he had to try.

"You have no business here, demon," Rusty said.

The creature's smile deepened. Its laugh was like a graveyard whisper—full of air but no substance.

"You have everything you need to find her, but remember, she'll remain with me for eternity if you cannot break the spell."

"Why are you doing this?" Rusty asked, trying a different way to distract the figure, hoping it would reveal something they could use to free Sherry. "Do I know you? Have I harmed you in some way?"

"No. I have nothing against you, or the woman. You have until midnight to find her or she'll belong to me forever, and your love will be nothing, as fragile as the paper on which the words are written."

Before Rusty could rush it, the figure disappeared.

Ruby and Rusty looked into the forest, but it was gone.

Sherry looked around her in confusion.

Where was she?

There was nothing but white around her, with long black lines on the walls that closed her in.

She wasn't standing on a floor, but neither was she floating in air. She stamped her feet and was relieved when nothing bad happened. There was air to breathe, but not fresh and smelled faintly of dust.

"Where am I?" Her voice sounded loud and scared to her ears.

"Hello?" she called out, but no one answered.

"Okay," she said to herself, "this is very strange."

She reached out to touch the walls around her and was surprised at the crinkly stiffness that met her fingertips.

"That feels like . . . paper," she said aloud. She punched at it, but the force of her fist merely crinkled the paper, and no amount of yanking on it or trying to pierce it with her nails made any difference to the surface.

Exhausted, Sherry sat on the floor of her prison and considered her situation.

Pinching herself to make sure she wasn't dreaming, she shook her head.

What had happened?

This couldn't be real.

But the bruise from her pinch was evidence it was very real indeed.

"Rusty," she said, "I need you."

Closing her eyes, she wished hard for him to hear her and find her.

Arriving back at the cabin, Rusty and Ruby headed straight to the letter, agreeing that there must be another clue there.

"I don't understand," Rusty said. His voice broke. "Why take Sherry?"

"She's human and defenseless," Ruby said. "I think it just needed a victim, and Sherry was perfect. She's kind and trusting. And she was desperate to find a gift for you that proved how much she loves you. She was ripe for plucking by this trickster spirit."

"I love her, Ruby. Without her, I am not sure I can go on."

"We'll get her back, Rusty. I promise."

She was studying the letter. Frowning in her concentration, she suddenly smiled.

"What time is it, Rusty?"

Rusty checked his watch and groaned. "We have ten minutes until midnight. Ten minutes. I don't know what to do."

Ruby squeezed his arm in comfort. "I think I know what to do, but you'll have to trust me." Ruby smiled. "The demon was right. The clues are all here. Sherry gave us the key to finding her in the letter, and the trickster confirmed it."

"How? What are you talking about? That demon gave us nothing."

"Oh, but it did." Ruby smiled. "Take a hold of the paper. No matter what happens, don't let go of it. Do exactly what I tell you, okay?"

"But you said . . ."

"I know what I told you before. You have to trust me. This is the only way. Say what I tell you to say, and do what I tell you to do without hesitation, okay?"

"For Sherry, I will do anything, even batter down the gates of hell if I have to," Rusty said.

Ruby waved her wand, muttering a quick spell that raised the paper and sent it to Rusty. "We'll hope that's not necessary, but I'm with you on that one. Take the paper, hold it tight. Don't let it go, no matter what happens, and repeat after me," she said.

Rusty took the paper in his hands and nearly let it go when the paper became lit with a white light that quickly became too bright to look at.

"Tell her how much you love her, Rusty."

Through the rushing wind that rose as the light increased its brightness, Rusty heard a cry that broke his heart—Sherry was calling him. He knew it was her.

"Sherry, I love you. I need you. Come back to me. Come back to me now."

Rusty professed his love without any prompting from Ruby, who stood nearby, chanting a spell that ripped the paper in two.

As suddenly as the light had been so bright it hurt the eyes, it left the room as the paper burst into flames, the letters of Sherry's profession of love lingering a moment in the air before turning to ash that quickly swirled and danced in the air before coalescing into a shape that landed on the floor at his feet.

Rusty gasped as Sherry rose, shaking the ash from her body.

Pulling her into his embrace, he held her close and whispered, "Welcome back, darling."

Sherry clung to him, tears mingling with his as they kissed.

"I love you," he said, taking her face in his hands and gazing into eyes he never thought he'd see again.

"I love you, too," Sherry whispered.

Ruby smiled. Packing her things back in her bag, she left, taking the stationery box with her to dispose of it properly when she returned home.

Later, cuddling in bed, Rusty explained what had happened, how they had found her missing and their subsequent search for her.

"I just wanted to find the perfect gift for you. When Ruby mentioned writing you a letter, I thought that would be the perfect present—a declaration of my love forever on paper for you to always see and know."

"It was. It is. But surely you already know you're the perfect present for me," Rusty said.

His hands stroking her hair and the kisses on her shoulder made it hard for Sherry to think, but her thoughts went back to Nikita at the shop, when she'd bought the paper.

"I think Nikita was right—there is magic in words. Just a little more magic than we expected. But the most magical words in the world are *I love you*," Sherry breathed into his ear as she wrapped her arms around him, and he pulled her closer.

Rusty didn't argue. As a matter of fact, he didn't speak intelligible words for quite a while, but she didn't mind. His actions spoke louder than his words ever could.

Read Sherry and Rusty's story in *Old Wounds* by Susan Burdorf

A FROST-MAS CAROL

BY AMY HALE

A Mills Family Christmas Story

I walked into the pawnshop and made my way to the back. The sound of my cane tapped loudly as I moved, and I enjoyed the way it echoed on the hardwood floors. The ornately carved wooden stick was my constant companion, and I loved that it announced my presence. Almost as if a herald running before me, warning others to step out of the way of the mighty Lawrence Mills.

And mighty I was. I might have been pushing two hundred years, and I know I looked frail, but there was still a fearsome frost dragon within these old bones that wouldn't hesitate to come forth if provoked. Lord almighty did this town provoke me. The people in this little valley vexed me to no end. Although often the other supernatural creatures that life had forced me to cohabitate with were just as bad.

I couldn't stand humans. They were selfish, ignorant, greedy, and weak. As a dragon, I understood appreciating wealth. I didn't become rich because I disliked money. But I also knew there was a line between self-preservation and greed. Careful consideration and proper justification should be in play before stepping over that boundary. I'd made that step a few times in my life, but each instance for the right reasons—to reach a long-term goal for the greater good. Humans just did it because they could and only thought of themselves.

I wasn't the town darling in Havenwood Falls, but I didn't care. I was happy being the old grouch that got things done, despite my lack of popularity. Or maybe because of my lack of popularity, I got things done. I rather enjoyed my fearsome notoriety, to tell the truth.

On this particular day, I was in a mood. I was going to have a chat with my son about his wasteful use of money on the Christmas decor at Simple Treasures Pawn Shop. He managed it, but I owned it. And I'd be damned if he'd blow a dime on such frivolousness without proper cause.

Tristan stepped out of the back room with a smile on his face, ready to greet his latest customer with his usual jovial demeanor. That grin died on his face as he saw me.

"Good morning. What can I do for you, Father?" He cleared his throat as he straightened some paperwork on the counter.

"Why does the outside of my shop look like a cheap holiday version of Disneyland?" I raised one bushy white eyebrow at him as I waited for his reply.

He didn't bother to look up at me. "It's two days before Christmas. It's generally tradition to decorate before and during the holiday. No one cares so much afterward."

"I don't care if it's the law; it's a wasteful use of money." I looked around at the sparkling trees, lights, and wreathes that dotted the decor. "It's almost as tacky in here. And what is that horrible commotion?"

Tristan stepped forward and put his hands on his hips. "It's Christmas music. This is the busiest buying season of the year. Christmas decor and music get people in the mood to spend money. Consider it an investment—like advertising."

"Advertising," I muttered. I pointed my cane in his direction. "It had darn well better pay off in spades. If we go in the red over some ridiculous baubles and animatronics, I'm taking it out of your salary."

Tristan shrugged. "Fine. Whatever makes you happy. But you will not destroy my personal enjoyment of the holiday. So huff and puff all you like."

I snorted. "That's the big bad wolf, you idiot. I eat those for breakfast."

He grinned. "So you say." He grabbed a package from the counter. "Is that all? I have things I need to do."

I nodded. "I suppose that will do for now."

The bell jingled over the door, and directly behind me I heard the distinct sound of two sets of footsteps. Human. I smelled a human. I pasted a less angry expression on my face, expecting to look a potential customer in the eyes.

"Hi, Grandpa." Zoey spoke softly as she grasped the hand of her human boyfriend, Jordan.

I looked down my nose at them both. "Zoey. Why are you not in school, girl?"

I didn't acknowledge Jordan.

"School is out. It's Christmas break." She spoke as if I should have already known this. Maybe I should have, but I rarely paid attention to such inconsequential things.

"Hmm." I eyed them both skeptically. "So what are you doing today?"

"Mom sent us to help Dad finish up any last-minute Christmas prep." Her eyes darted past me, and when I turned to look, I caught Tristan finishing up a signal to stop talking.

"I see." I turned back to face her. "Well, carry on then."

While I didn't like her boyfriend, I marginally adored my granddaughter. I would occasionally make concessions for her. If it made her happy, I could allow for a smidge more Christmas decorating. But only a smidge.

"Behave yourselves." I gave a pointed look to the blond jock fawning over my granddaughter. My daughter-in-law Bianca may be human, but she should've known better than to encourage Zoey's interest in this human male. I'd made it clear frequently that we needed her to marry a frost dragon to keep the family line as pure as possible. It seemed another reminder was in order.

I left the building and glanced at my watch. It was just after one in the afternoon, and I hadn't yet stopped for lunch. I got in my car and drove up the mountain to Fallview Tavern & Grille. They made a great steak, had good bourbon, and my daughter Jetta sang there and at Haven Saloon as the entertainment. With any luck, I'd run into her. She'd pretty much cut me off after I disapproved of her choice of husbands, but she'd eventually see the error of her ways. I was always right. She'd discover that the hard way, I supposed.

The entry way of Fallview was a stark contrast to the bright sunlit day just outside the doors. I'd always enjoyed the atmospheric darkness of this building. It reminded me of the caves we'd once inhabited before we considered houses proper lodging for shifters like us.

"Mr. Mills. Good to see you." A voice from the bar beckoned me closer. It was Simon, Fallview's chief cook and bartender. He was also a dragon shifter, but the ordinary fire kind—several notches below the majestic frost dragons. "Can I get you a drink?"

I nodded. "Don't lie, Simon. No one is ever happy to see me. A bourbon would be fine. And I'm going to order lunch, so I'll take a menu as well."

Simon smirked as he passed me a menu. Moments later he slid my drink in front of me as I took in my surroundings. Once again, I felt disgust at the festive display. People were like sheep. They followed whatever trends were popular and partook in tradition simply for the sake of it—solid logic and reasoning be damned. Sadly, this holiday thing had yet to fade into the background.

"What are you doing here?" Jetta sat next to me at the bar and motioned for Simon to get her a drink. Her many piercings reflected the Christmas lights behind the bar, and I rolled my eyes at both abominations.

"Having a drink and lunch." I kept my eyes on the menu, although I already knew what I was ordering.

"That's all? No hidden agenda or plan to sabotage my life again?" She downed a shot of whiskey.

"Despite our differences, I only want the best for you, Jetta," I replied.

"Uh-huh. And I'm a fucking virgin." She motioned for Simon to hit her again.

I sighed. "You always have to be so repulsive and undignified. I'll never understand it. That's not how I raised you."

She chuckled. "Exactly. I want to be nothing like you, so to assure that, I do the opposite. Cursing, tattoos, piercings, tight clothes, lots of sex, loud music, and a shitload of happiness. That's me being nothing like you."

I changed the subject, knowing the current conversation would go nowhere.

"So how is . . ." I waved my hand in circles, trying to summon his name.

"Conrad. His name is Conrad, and you damn well know it, you prickly asshole." She slammed her drink on the bar. "He's fantastic. I'm fantastic. You're not welcome here. You can leave now." She slid off the barstool and moved to the stage, where she began fiddling with her guitar.

I shook my head as I sipped my drink. Her frustration with me was petty. I'd tried to control certain aspects of her life, but it was always for her own good. I'd only ever wanted to do what was best for her and the family. Sadly, now the Mills pedigree was not only tainted with human blood but also lava dragon blood. The disgrace was almost more than I could bear.

At that thought, I lost my appetite, so I finished my drink and paid Simon. I'd have to work on that problem another day. The Court expected me to finalize the flower selection and preparations for the Cold Moon Ball, and I needed something to cheer me up if I were to deal cordially with that ninny fae at the flower shop.

A visit to the cave would be good for me. I hadn't been there in quite some time, and I needed to feel grounded in the truth of my being. A reminder of my ancestors and their origins would help me keep a proper perspective. Despite the hike required to reach it, I was looking forward to my alone time there. I wasn't as feeble as most people thought, and the hike only slightly winded me.

Once I reached Smalls Falls, I stepped into the dark cavern hidden behind it and smiled. The damp, cold air was invigorating and a refreshing balm to my old soul. I was a frost dragon, and the cold was simply a part of who I was. The chill in the air was like an old friend.

I gazed around me at the sparkling walls, full of diamonds waiting to be plucked from the earth. If humans knew of this place, it would have been stripped empty years ago, but we dragons knew how to save our riches and appreciate them. There'd only been one human that I knew of in this cave, and thanks to a powerful cloaking spell, all he saw was a small, dark, dirty opening. Only dragons can enter the true heart of the cave and see it for what it really is.

Surrounded by my treasures, I sat in solitude and smiled.

A huge blizzard had been forecast for Havenwood Falls, and the storm began shortly after I left the cave. Normally a night like that would calm my nerves, but my rest that night was fitful. I had an array of odd dreams that all mashed together. The common theme, though, was very Charles Dickens-like. I was to be visited by three ghosts so I could learn and change my ways. Ha! My ways were just fine and had not only allowed me to be one of the wealthiest members in our society, but had also kept my seat on the Court of the Sun and the Moon.

Those ghosts never appeared in my dreams, though. I supposed even my subconscious knew there was no reason to waste their time. Lawrence Mills didn't need changing.

Upon awakening, I opened my eyes and felt an odd sensation of floating wash over me. The room spun, and bright colors flashed for a split-second before all appeared normal again. I rubbed my face, trying to wipe away what had to be the remnants of a dream.

"Wake up, my love," a soft feminine voice whispered in my ear.

I sat up quickly, inspecting the room around me. I needed to determine if I was still half asleep. I must have been, for I was alone in the room and that voice very much resembled the sound of my long dead wife.

I shook off the thought and prepared for a busy day. Once downstairs, I fully expected there to be people hard at work prepping our ballroom for the event I reluctantly hosted every year. To my surprise, it was quiet and empty.

Christmas was tomorrow and the ball just four days later. There was no way my assistants had taken the day off. They knew better. I'd already granted them Christmas Day off, and slacking on

Christmas Eve was unacceptable. I didn't enjoy doing all this, but I took the responsibility seriously and never allowed for idle hands or cut corners.

I made my way into the dining room to find my breakfast placed at my setting. My housekeeper stood beside the table, ready to serve me.

"Where is everyone?" I muttered as I took my seat.

She poured my coffee. "Everyone, sir?"

I knit my brows together. "The people I hired to prep for the ball."

I took a bite of my eggs. She didn't answer, so I raised my eyes to hers.

"I . . . I have no idea, sir." She kept her expression passive, but I could sense a hint of confusion in her voice.

"Never mind. You may go." I waved her away as I stabbed a slice of ham with my fork.

She nodded and quickly left the room. I ate my breakfast in silence, and still I waited for the usual sounds of holiday chaos to assault my ears. Nothing. It was so quiet, the only thing I could hear was my breathing.

I enjoyed my peace and solitude, but this absence of productivity had an eerie feeling about it. I tossed my napkin on my plate, determined to get to the bottom of my helpers' absences. I dialed my primary assistant, Greg, but the number wasn't working.

"Strange," I muttered.

I needed to go into town, so I would just stop by his office instead. My guess was all the resources had been diverted to preparing for that vampire Michela's stupid wedding. I'd have to have a talk with her about that. I didn't tolerate my usual help being poached.

As I drove down my street, I noticed an absence of Christmas decor on the neighbors' houses.

"That's odd," I said to myself. "Those homes were all lit up just yesterday. I'm sure of it."

The farther I drove, the more confused I became. Everyone had removed their holiday decorations. Not a single strand of lights remained. And while that's a revelation that would normally please me, I couldn't help but feel unease.

Another question plagued my mind. *Where was all the snow?* The blizzard was supposed to have produced massive accumulation by now. My Land Rover would normally make it into town with only a minor amount of struggle, but surprisingly, that wasn't a necessary worry now. The forecasters were idiots and could never get anything right.

When I entered the town square, I felt my breath catch. It was as if they had stripped away all the hard work of the last couple of weeks with the snap of one's fingers. My eyes immediately went to the pawn shop. All the bright, annoying, animatronic holiday figures had disappeared. I didn't miss them, but I also felt like I was losing my mind. I needed answers.

I parked and marched inside. The interior was just as humdrum and quiet as the outside. I slammed my cane on the hardwood floor, and the echo was almost deafening.

"What in the blazes is going on here?" I shouted into the empty store.

Tristan came running out from the back. "Father? Are you okay?"

"Where are all the Christmas decorations you so adamantly declared were necessary just twenty-four hours ago?" I bellowed.

He frowned. "What are you talking about?"

"It's Christmas Eve, you idiot. Why did you take down all the —" I waved my hands around the room, trying to find the words to adequately describe the chaos I'd disapproved of the previous day.

"The what?" Tristan watched me warily.

"The decorations! Where are all the disgustingly cheerful decorations?"

He eyed me with suspicion. "We've never decorated the shop for the holidays. You've never allowed it. Are you feeling okay?"

I slammed my cane down again. "Dammit, boy, don't test my patience."

"Do you want me to call your doctor?" He stepped toward me.

"Where is Zoey? She'll know what I'm talking about." I stuck my nose in the air, sure the girl would clear up the little joke being played.

64

"Zoey? Who's Zoey?" He sighed. "You're not making any sense."

Pretending we'd never had a discussion about decorations was one thing, but denying the existence of my only granddaughter was going too far. "Your daughter. Don't pretend you don't know your own daughter. I've had quite enough of this game!"

Tristan ran a hand through his hair. "I don't have a daughter. And it's cruel of you to pretend otherwise." His tone softened. "You know how badly I wanted a family."

"Bianca would hardly find that amusing." I huffed.

"Bianca?" He stepped forward. "Bianca!" His voice increased in volume. "You ran Bianca out of town over twenty years ago. I haven't seen nor heard from her since. You are the reason I'm still alone all these years later."

I looked him in the eyes. Studied him. *Had he lost his mind?* Yes, I'd tried to run Bianca off when he told me he wanted to marry her, but it hadn't worked. No matter how much I offered her, or what blackmail I'd tried to use, she'd refused to leave his side. They'd married and moved away instead, only recently moving back. Their daughter Zoey was the only worthwhile thing that came out of that marriage.

"You know as well as I do that plan of mine didn't work." I sneered at him, reminded once again of how weak human emotions had made us.

He shook his head, and a tear ran down his cheek. "If only that were true." He wiped his face and turned to go back to the office. "If you want decorations, put them up yourself. I don't care. I hate this time of year."

I almost stumbled backward at the disbelief of his words. He didn't hate Christmas. He adored it to a sickening extent. *What in the hell was going on around this town?*

I left the shop without another word. My mind reeled at the possibility that I'd somehow gotten the perfect Christmas, which was no Christmas at all.

But Zoey. *Where was my lovely, innocent granddaughter?*

A voice called to me from across the street. I looked up to see a beautiful woman in a long blue dress, her dark hair flowing freely down her back. As she crossed to meet me, I froze in my tracks.

"Christine?" I gasped. "It can't be!"

My long-deceased wife stepped on to the curb, looking as lovely as I'd ever seen her. My hand gripped my cane to the point I was afraid I'd snap the head off.

"Hello, Lawrence." Her sweet voice echoed around me, entered my very being, and stabbed me in the heart.

"How?" I stammered. "Where did you come from?"

She dusted a small bit of lint from the shoulder of my jacket. "I'm a ghost, silly man."

I shook my head. "This isn't possible."

She laughed, and as it always did, the sound warmed my soul. "We're in Havenwood Falls. Anything is possible." She gestured to Whisper Falls Inn. "Shoot, you have a ghost living there. Why is my appearance so inconceivable?"

"You didn't want to stay. You moved on when you passed." I couldn't help the slight hint of resentment and pain that filled my words.

"I did. I had no unfinished business here. But obviously you and your poor attitude have become my business." She sighed.

"My attitude." I chuckled. "You haven't been around to give me an annual adjustment, so you only have yourself to blame."

She smiled. "Oh, I promise to rectify that as soon as possible." She grabbed my ear and pulled me to her. I howled in pain as she held me there. "I woke you up this morning to drag your sorry behind through this parallel world. A world you *think* you'd prefer. You listen to me, Lawrence James Mills, you have the rest of today to figure this out or the changes you see around you will be permanent in your own dimension." She pushed me away from her in disgust.

"Changes? So this is really happening?" I let my eyes roam the rest of the square, noting the absolute somberness that surrounded us.

"It is. But for now, only in this sphere." She glared at me. "You've already seen two consequences of your actions. Bianca was a huge part of the Havenwood Falls decorating committee, but thanks to you, she doesn't even live here. No one else was willing to take you on and fight your stance against celebrating the holidays.

And our son. Just look at how sad and lonely our son is. There will be no one to carry on the Mills family legacy thanks to you."

I shrugged. "He's probably better off. There's still Jetta."

I would not admit that not having Zoey left an ache in my heart I couldn't describe.

Christine frowned. "Oh, dear. You are far worse than I imagined."

She paced.

"What?" I asked. "I know the child's name wouldn't be Mills, but since Conrad is at least a dragon, it would still be a mostly pure heritage." Yes, I was settling, but it was better than nothing.

Christine's sad face faded from my view. "It's not that simple anymore."

"Wait!" I reached for her as she dissipated before my eyes.

"Jetta." I whispered her name, wondering what could have possibly changed about her life. She was too stubborn to let my machinations get in her way.

I drove to the little house she shared with her husband Conrad and rang the doorbell. An elderly woman opened the door.

"Oh, hello." I could barely hear her timid voice. "How can I help you?"

I frowned.

"Where is Jetta?" I asked bluntly.

"Jetta?" She echoed in confusion.

"Jetta Mills, or rather Jetta Monroe. My daughter." I leaned into my cane as I drew closer to the woman.

She shook her head. "I can't say I know." She held up one finger. "Wait. I know a Jetta Ireland. She lives in a delightful house over in Creekwood."

"Ireland?" I repeated.

The woman nodded.

"Thank you, ma'am." I turned on my heel and quickly re-entered my car to find my daughter.

Is it possible? Did Jetta end up with Turner after all? I was almost giddy at the thought. Finally, something good had gone as planned.

I drove slowly through the neighborhood until I saw her Jeep in the driveway of an impressive two-story home. Finally, she was living in a home fitting of the Mills name.

I pulled in the drive just as Turner was leaving the house.

"Lawrence! So good to see you!" His jubilant greeting was a surprising breath of fresh air in a town that no longer seemed interested in being joyful.

I patted him on the back. "It's good to see you, too, my boy. Is Jetta home?"

He turned to the door. "Sure."

He took a few steps back to the door, opened it, and yelled for her. Jetta appeared moments later. I hardly recognized her. She was wearing a pink and white blouse and skirt ensemble. She no longer wore her beautiful silver hair in the pixie cut she usually sported. It was long and pulled back into barrettes on the sides. Her face was absent of makeup, and I could see no visible tattoos or piercings. She looked tired.

"Yes, Turner?" Her voice was soft as she answered him.

"Your father is here to see you." He waved her forward, and she tentatively stepped toward us.

She raised her eyes to mine. "Hello, Daddy."

Daddy? She hadn't called me that since she was a little girl.

"Hello, Jetta. I wanted to stop by and see if you were doing any Christmas songs at the bar this year." I didn't care about Christmas music, but I needed an excuse to check on her. And if I were totally honest, I somewhat enjoyed her music, not that I'd ever admit it to her.

"Songs? I don't really do Karaoke." Her eyes quickly shifted between Turner and me.

"Not Karaoke, silly girl. Your job at Fallview. Or maybe at Haven Saloon this year."

She shifted and looked uncomfortable. "I don't have a job at either place. I haven't played music in years. Not since . . ." She glanced at Turner, who was now looking for something in his car.

"You gave up your music?" It surprised me to hear this. Music had been her life.

"Turner preferred I focus on our relationship and our home." She smiled ever so slightly, but I could see there was no genuine joy in her expression.

I shifted my attention to Turner. *Let's settle the legacy situation, at least.* "So when are you two going to give me some grandkids?"

Jetta frowned. Turner chuckled. "Ah, we've decided that's not the route for us." He polished a spot on his Lexus. "I can't take a chance on losing her gorgeous figure. Besides, kids are messy."

I realized my jaw was hanging open. I'd always known Turner was full of himself, but this was beyond belief. He'd turned Jetta into a submissive shell of who she really was. And while she was often a pain in my ass, I secretly appreciated aspects of her independence. Regardless of her choices, which I rarely approved of, I knew that Jetta would never be taken advantage of. I didn't have to worry about her. But this version of her was hard to grasp. To my amazement, I didn't like her this way at all. Not even as much as the former version. And no kids? Jetta didn't seem thrilled with Turner's selfish explanation. I didn't remember her ever wanting kids, but I'd always expected them. I'd believed she'd eventually want a family of her own.

I looked at Jetta again, and she just stared at Turner. Something wasn't right between them. It's not the way I envisioned her marriage to Turner at all.

"I'll let you two get back to what you were doing." I turned back to my car.

"Daddy?" Jetta called out to me.

I turned my head to look at her. "Yes?"

She opened her mouth, but then looked at Turner and closed it. "Nothing. Have a good day."

I nodded. "You, too."

A good day. I wasn't sure that was possible at this point.

My thoughts were spinning so fast my head hurt.

"The Cave," I whispered. I needed to get my bearings again. I could do it there.

In a matter of minutes, I was once again at the entrance of my favorite place on earth. I stepped inside, but the usual shine that surrounded me was dim.

"Not quite so pretty now, huh?" Christine's voice materialized beside me, followed by the rest of her.

I looked at her. "What happened?"

She put her hands on her hips. "What do you think happened?"

I stretched my hand out and ran it along one of the dirt walls. "My diamonds. They're gone." A low, feral growl entered my voice. "Humans."

Rage turned my vision red.

She placed a hand on my arm. "Humans can't get in here, remember?"

I shook my head.

"Then who?" I huffed out angry breaths.

Christine tilted her head and stared at me as if I were a fool.

I quickly realized she was right. "Dragons? But only our family knows of this place."

"And who in our family would be dumb enough to mine it almost empty?" She crossed her arms.

I thought on that a moment. Who indeed? Tristan and Jetta never cared for money. Bianca didn't either, but she was out of this particular picture. That just left— "Turner."

Christine nodded. "He's always been after Jetta's money. Your money. When he married her, some moron let him have free rein as long as they were together."

I swallowed hard as I remembered the offer I'd made to Turner if he successfully broke up Jetta and Conrad. He would get access to Jetta's half of the inheritance now. *But would he stoop so low as to steal from our cave?* It appeared so.

"Lawrence, you've seen a small sample of what your ideal world has created. Now you have to ask yourself if you are selfish enough to leave it as it is, or change it back to how it should be."

I didn't know what to say. I didn't like the way things were in the old dimension, but I hated this more.

"It should go back," I stated flatly.

"Good. Now, how are you going to make that happen?" She looked me in the eye.

"I have no idea," I replied.

My tires screeched to a halt as I pulled into Jetta and Turner's driveway. I was beyond angry. I was shifting mad. I hopped out of the car, leaving my cane in the passenger seat.

"Turner! Get out here now!" My voice echoed like a clap of thunder as my inner dragon threatened to surface.

In moments, he and Jetta were in the front yard.

I pointed a boney finger in his direction. "You selfish, greedy, unfeeling thief!"

"Excuse me?" His eyes narrowed at my accusation.

"You not only stole the diamonds right out of our family cave, but you've taken advantage of my daughter's good nature." I stepped closer and pulled at the sleeve of her pink blouse. "What is this? This isn't Jetta. What have you done to her?"

Jetta opened her mouth, but a withering look from Turner caused her to snap her jaw shut.

"Oh, no." I stood before her now. "You will not allow this selfish coward to silence or bully you any longer."

Tears formed on her lashes.

"Say what you need to say, girl. Tell him," I demanded.

"Turner," she whispered, "I hate you." Her voice gained some gusto then. "I hate you so fucking much that it makes my teeth ache just looking at you."

I nodded in approval.

"Hey, you can't talk to me that—"

I stepped forward and poked a finger in his chest. I began to see the world in muted shades of green, and Turner's expression of fear meant he knew I was on the verge of shifting.

Jetta gathered her courage more. "You took away everything I loved. My music, my individuality, and my self-expression died because you couldn't handle me thinking for myself. I'm tired of being your perfect wife."

I nodded again, encouraging her to continue.

She smiled as she slipped the ring off her hand and tossed it at him. "I'm filing for divorce. And since we have a prenuptial agreement, you won't end up with jack shit."

I applauded. "Well done, girl. Go see my attorney right after Christmas. I'll cover all expenses."

Turner paled. "Now wait. You can't—"

"I can't what?" I roared. "I am a founding member of this community. I am patriarch of the Mills family and all the fortunes that go with it." I paused and leaned in close for effect.

"And I am the father of the woman you are taking advantage of."

Turner looked at me, and I could still see a tinge of fear in his eyes. "I recommend you take what you came with and get out of Havenwood Falls. Send a forwarding address for the legal paperwork when you get back to whatever hole you crawled out of. And never darken our town with your presence again."

"Or what?" he challenged me.

"Or I will assure the name Turner Ireland is obliterated from history. No one will find your body or miss you, let alone speak your name ever again." The genuine anger I felt was almost as surprising to me as it was to Jetta and Turner. "You will no longer exist."

He turned and stumbled off into the house. I put a hand on Jetta's shoulder.

"Let me know if he hesitates to do as he's told. I'll come back and light a bigger fire under his butt."

She nodded, and I faced my car, ready to leave.

"Daddy?" she whispered.

I faced her. "Yes, Jetta?"

She pulled me to her in a genuine hug, and I heard a sob escape as she tried to speak. "Thank you for believing in me and standing up for me."

I pulled back and nodded, unsure what to do with this affection. I hadn't gotten that kind of response from her since she was little. I'd never been good with it, to be honest, but at least when she was little, I expected it.

I pulled out my handkerchief and wiped her tears. "You take care of yourself and do not put up with any more of that boy's shenanigans." I paused. "Or mine, for that matter. Make your own way and push to the side anyone standing as an obstacle. They don't deserve to be in your life."

I thought of the Jetta I knew before. The Jetta that kicked me out of her life for trying to stop her marriage.

"Even me," I whispered. I deserved her hatred. I could see that now.

I left, hoping to catch Tristan before he closed the shop.

"That was a good thing you just did, Lawrence." Christine materialized in the seat next to me.

I shrugged. "I suppose."

She patted my leg. "You know darn well it was. You just have a hard time admitting that you might actually love your family."

"Love is a weakness that gets you taken advantage of. Look at how Turner used Jetta's love against her?"

She shook her head. "She wasn't supposed to end up with Turner. I feel sure Conrad would never stoop to such a level."

"Hmph." I didn't care for the boy, but she was probably right there.

"What do you plan to do now?" She smiled at me.

"I need to help Tristan."

I pulled into a parking space in front of the pawn shop and quickly went inside.

Tristan was standing next to an older woman, helping her with her purchases.

"We need to talk," I announced.

He looked up at me and frowned. "I think we did enough talking earlier." He handed a large bag to the woman. "Do you need help getting this to your car?"

She shook her head. "I got it. Thank you."

He smiled at her, and I watched her scurry past me, obviously eager to be out of my presence.

"You need Bianca," I stated. "I don't have to like it, but it's the truth."

He leaned against the counter. "Too little, too late there."

"Nonsense. It's never too late. We can find her and bring her back." The boy was obviously not thinking straight. It didn't have to be difficult.

He sighed. "I know you have a lot of tricks up that sleeve of yours, but unless you can bring someone back from the dead, we don't have a snowball's chance in hell."

I lost my balance for a moment and had to steady my cane. "What do you mean?"

"Bianca died in a car accident last year. Her husband was drunk and driving too fast. They hit a tree." He wiped a tear from his eye. "It's too late."

He grabbed his coat and rushed past me. "I'm going home. Feel free to lock up."

I stood there, alone with my thoughts. And again I found myself not liking the self-reflection.

If Bianca had stayed in Havenwood Falls, she'd still be alive. She'd be here, making Tristan happy and taking care of my granddaughter Zoey.

Zoey.

The thought of her never being born brought a tear to my eye. I was used to anger, frustration, and apathy. But this emotion was one I hadn't felt since Christine died. Grief. I felt the loss of someone who'd never been born, but should have.

I locked up the shop and walked over to the park. The gazebo used to be one of Zoey's favorite spots, so I took a seat inside and let the shock wash over me. *Was it too late? Had I really botched this all up so badly that it couldn't be fixed?*

"Go home, Lawrence. There's nothing more you can do here," Christine whispered softly near my ear.

"I . . ." The words wouldn't form. "This isn't how it's supposed to be!" I shouted, and my voice cracked with sorrow.

"This is what happens when you try to run other people's lives. You end up with less and less control over the outcome." She stood and pointed at me with accusation in her features. "You made your bed. Now lie in it!" she shouted.

I dropped my cane to the wooden floor and covered my face with my hands. "No. No, there has to be something I can do! Please tell me I can take it all back. I want to take it all back!"

I curled up on the bench seat and closed my eyes, the guilt and grief hitting me in waves that left me almost breathless. I was drowning in it.

I gasped for air, feeling as if an icy stiff hand were around my throat. I opened my eyes to see Christine's angry face before me. "You have disappointed me, Lawrence darling. You could have done better."

Flashes of color surrounded me, and once again I felt the odd sensation of floating.

"I will!" I bolted to a sitting position only to find I was in my bed. I grasped the covers in my fists, trying to assure myself that they were real. "I'm home."

I slid out of bed and tried to make sense of it all. *Was it all a dream? Had my sweet Christine visited me in my sleep? Did I really visit a parallel universe?*

I quickly dressed, not bothering to comb my wild white hair, which was likely standing on end all over my head. Jetta had often remarked I resembled a mad scientist when I first awoke. The thought made me smile a little.

I hurried out the door, despite the protests of my housekeeper. It thrilled me to see that my neighborhood was covered in all the festive trimmings of the season and a generous amount of snow covered the ground. I would never like the holidays myself, but I would no longer begrudge another's joy in them.

I drove down the hill into town, my eyes searching frantically for any sign that life in Havenwood Falls was as it should be. The pawn shop was closed for Christmas, so I drove to Tristan's house. I didn't even bother to knock as I burst through the front door.

"Tristan," I called.

The living room was full of my family. Bianca looked shocked to see me. "Lawrence? Did you change your mind and decide to join us after all?"

"Shit," came a reply from the kitchen as Jetta stepped into view. She was wearing a black and red outfit that would normally make me apoplectic, but all I could do was smile. Her hair was short, she was half naked, and all her tattoos and piercings were in place. *Perfect.*

Zoey approached me cautiously. "Are you okay, Grandpa?"

I looked into her face, and a tear slid down my cheek. I grabbed her and pulled her in for a hug.

Everyone in the room looked at each other in confusion.

Tristan put a hand on my back. "Are you drunk?"

I shook my head. "Not at all."

Zoey pulled back and looked up at me. "Are you okay?"

I smiled. "Better than I have been in a long time."

She squeezed me tight. "Merry Christmas, Grandpa."

I knew I had a lot of things to account for, and there were many things I still didn't understand or particularly like, but I would worry about those things tomorrow. Today was a day to be thankful. I didn't hesitate in my reply. "Merry Christmas, everyone."

"Merry Christmas, Lawrence." Christine's voice echoed through my soul.

"Merry Christmas, Christine. Thank you," I whispered.

Have you read all the Mills family stories by Amy Hale?
Somewhere Within
Flames Among the Frost
Betrayal Among the Frost

THE HEART OF CHRISTMAS

BY KALLIE ROSS

A Kasun Family Christmas Story

"Merry Christmas," Conall Kasun's tired voice announced his arrival home early Christmas morning. It had been a long night, and he'd mustered as much enthusiasm as he could to greet his family. He pulled at his khaki shirt and loosened his belt. The familiar deputy uniform was rarely seen in such disarray. Patrolling their magical town had to be done, especially at night, and the holidays were always a little more magical. The Christmas decorations lended to the whimsy, but the town's supernatural inhabitants had always added more than their usual *charm* to this season.

Conall Kasun, one of Havenwood Falls' finest, would have much rather spent the cold winter night guarding the border of the town with his brother in wolf form, but due to the blizzard and all the trouble it had caused, he'd been out on official police business. Working on Christmas Eve wasn't ideal. Conall had simply been thankful to be home after dealing with the snow, frantic tourists, and local drama. His wolf pack duties were so much less tempestuous than the recent town circumstances.

The Kasun Pack had spent over three hundred years protecting the magic pouring out of the mystically hidden falls. For 150 of those years, Conall had patrolled alongside his family, witnessing the wildest escapades, preventing age-old rivalries from evolving into all-out wars, and assisting good defeat evil time after time. In the early 1700s, Gaby and Ric Kasun led their wolf pack disguised as Native Americans. Through the years, their efforts had evolved into the town's local law enforcement. Conall had even grown to enjoy putting on his uniform for a night shift when it meant he could spend an uninterrupted Christmas Day with his family.

"Hey, Daddy," an adorable brown-eyed girl with dimples answered. "Look at what I added." Morgan smiled and waved her hands in front of her at all of the Christmas decorations, but they all looked the same as when he'd left the night before.

So Conall took a closer look at Morgan, hoping she would give him a clue. She was growing up too fast. Her eyes darted to the fireplace, and suddenly Conall found what she wanted to share. She'd drawn a picture of their house, surrounded by forest, with a red stick figure waving from the chimney. She'd taped it to the mantle next to where her stocking hung. Conall adored how much Morgan loved Christmas. The only other person who might have loved the holiday more was her mother.

As Conall released the clasp on his belt, his eyes traveled from the tree trimmed in handmade ornaments across the room to the garland-clad handrails leading upstairs. There wasn't a surface untouched by red, green, or glitter. Conall's heavy leather holster swung around his body and landed on a lumpy plaid blanket laid over the couch.

"Hey!" a pre-teen voice growled, with a hint of intimidation, from under the belt. Connor's eyes were shut tight as he pulled the blanket off his head and one earbud out from under his shaggy brown hair. "Watch it."

"Maybe you should watch your tone," Conall replied dryly. It had only been last year that his son bounced in the room with the same excitement Morgan exuded.

Hormones. Connor would be experiencing his first shift soon. The year leading up to any shifter's first transformation was riddled with angst and sarcasm, but it didn't excuse Connor's disrespect.

Both of Connor's eyes opened in shock. "Sorry, Dad." He sat up to make room for his dad's duty belt, complete with handcuffs, keys, radio, knife, flashlight, and gun. As the belt replaced Connor's head on the cushion, the twelve-year-old not only noticed the tired, dark circles under his father's eyes, but the worried brow and frown. "What's got you in a mood?"

Morgan placed a hand on her hip and defended, "We could ask you the same thing."

Conall and Connor glanced at each other in awe of Morgan's sass, but neither of them were entirely surprised. Quick wit and an even quicker tongue were two traits every Kasun seemed to be born with. Morgan may have been cute enough to be in a Gap commercial, but not unlike her father, she spoke her mind and questioned everything. Recently, after turning five, her curiosity had shifted into inquiry, and Conall noted that every time they had a conversation, he felt like he was in an interview room at the station.

"I'm too tired for an interrogation," Conall said before a yawn escaped him. "Where's your mother?"

"She's looking for your special ornament," Connor grumbled and moved to put his earbud back in place. "Supposedly, it's vanished."

With supernatural reflexes, Conall caught Connor's hand before he could shut the world out with whatever he binge-watched online. "No more Connor-time. It's family time." Conall nodded in the direction of Connor's room. "Go put those up and meet us in the kitchen for breakfast."

Conall signaled to Morgan like she was one of the other deputies, pointing her in the direction she should go with his hand. She gave a silent nod, then swiftly and silently ran into the next room. Connor, on the other hand, peeled the blanket off his lap, sending his phone clattering to the hardwood floor, and let out a groan as his long limbs clumsily straightened themselves.

"What are you up to?" he asked suspiciously.

Conall shrugged. "Today we are at the mercy of your mother and her Christmas spirit."

"I don't think she's going to want to move on to brunch and presents until she's found that ornament," Connor said, and he was probably right. He walked in the direction of the stairs, but paused at the bottom.

"Merry Christmas, babe, and happy anniversary." Millie smiled as she made her way down two steps at a time. Connor stepped to the side and let his mother pass before leaving the way she came. Recently, his parents' affectionate greetings had become unbearably embarrassing.

Conall wrapped his arms around Millie and kissed her.

"Oooooh," Morgan called as she leaned through the kitchen doorway. "Daddy, what am I supposed to be doing in here?"

"We all need to keep looking for that ornament," Millie said as she pointed to the tree. "I can't imagine what happened to it. I swear I hung it in the usual spot."

"Hmm," Conall attempted to sound just as puzzled as she was. "When was the last time you think you saw it?"

"Yesterday. I distinctly remember seeing it as I placed a few presents under the tree," she answered.

"Maybe it fell into the tree or down behind a gift," Conall offered. "We'll find it later once they all have been cleared out."

Millie shook her head and said, "But that won't be until later, after dinner. And with both our families crammed into the living room, someone might step on it and break it."

"How about I promise to do a deep dive into, under, and even behind the tree before everyone comes over?" Conall asked, then dotted a kiss on Millie's cheek. "I'd really love some Christmas pancakes. I'm starving."

"I'm starving, too," Connor said as he hesitantly made his way down the stairs. "Are you two done?"

"Never," Millie declared, and she took Conall in her arms and kissed him dramatically.

Conall laughed, and they moved toward the kitchen together. He would have to think of something pretty special to get his wife's mind off that ornament. Considering it was their thirtieth wedding anniversary and he'd proposed to Millie holding the now-missing ornament, it would be impossible to distract her merely with pancakes. But Conall knew something Millie and the kids didn't: the ornament wasn't missing at all. He'd hidden it in one of the wrapped presents under the tree with a special gift inside.

"I know . . . while we're making brunch, I'll tell the story of how we met," Conall said.

"Yay!" Morgan encouraged.

Connor grumbled something unintelligible.

Millie grinned and added, "That is one of my top five favorite Christmases."

They all made themselves comfortable around the kitchen island. The children sat on stools on one end across from where Conall and Millie worked in tandem to prepare pancake batter. Conall retrieved the bowl and utensils while Millie gathered the ingredients from the refrigerator. They made sharing a life look easy and fun, but it hadn't always been easy.

"So it was 1988, and neon was overrated," Conall started as he cracked the first egg against a white mixing bowl.

"Wait a second," Morgan interrupted and waved a hand in the air. "That's not how a story starts. You gotta say *once upon a time.*"

Conall tilted his head in confusion. "But it's not that kind of story. It's a true, ah, um . . ."

Millie coughed softly to catch Conall's attention. "It was that kind of story for me," she said, and nudged him with her elbow. "And someday, I hope Morgan and Connor will be able to tell a similar story about how they met the love of their life."

Conall smiled and gave her a nod of understanding. Their story might not have been a fairytale by Disney-standards, but it was magical.

"Once upon a time . . ." Conall began again.

There was a dashing, young wolf shifter living in a small Colorado town. That's me. I'd finished patrolling at the town border, but on four paws, not in my patrol car. Back in the 80s, I worked the front desk at the station on the weekdays. Things weren't much different in Havenwood Falls, but as I mentioned previously, there was an abundance of neon, and for some reason all the girls had really big hair.

At the time, I lived with my parents in their cabin up the road. You know it as Grandpa Ric's house. Our house wasn't even built yet. Of course, your Grandma Gaby was still with us. I wish you two could have met her. She was special. Like your mom, she came from far away, and the minute she stepped into this canyon, she knew she belonged.

That Friday was the Cold Moon Ball. We still had the feast at the community center, then went to Mills mansion for the dancing and donations. I had three priorities before the party started. First, to get a Christmas gift for my girlfriend at the time. Second, to man the desk for my shift at the station. Third, to get dressed up for the ball and make sure my girlfriend had a good time, but not a great time, because I had plans to break up with her three days later, after Christmas. Kat Gregs and I had dated off and on for a couple years, but it had never felt right.

Your uncle Tate had a rule for dating seasonally, and according to him, I'd missed my window to break up with Kat. You know, he never tried to convince your uncle Kase to follow this rule, but I have a feeling it's because he realized he didn't want anyone to treat your aunt Willa that way. Back then, though, we didn't have any sisters to know better. Anyway, until meeting your aunt Alex, Tate only dated casually after February 14th, and made sure to end things in early November. He said it kept relationships from getting messy, and it was the year I met your mother his theory proved to be correct.

The square downtown had been my best bet at finding a gift, so that's where I headed first. The family store received a new shipment of ski apparel, and a quilted vest seemed like the easiest and least personal gift I could buy Kat. As I drove into town, finding a parking spot close to the storefront seemed impossible, then suddenly someone backed out of a spot in front of Howe's Herbal Shoppe, and I pulled in.

The store looked just like it does now, with Havenwood Falls souvenirs lining the shelves up front and all of Ruby Howe's talismans and home remedies in the back. Ruby wasn't quite as kooky as she comes across now, but she still had a funny way of talking. It was like she was putting a spell on me as she coaxed me inside with the promise of hot cider and the perfect gift for Kat.

Ms. Howe, in her whimsical way, led me through the store pointing out candles, hand-made dream catchers, and even hinted at selling me a bundle of herbs that would spice up my love life. I explained it was the last thing I needed, and while she bent down to rummage through a drawer behind her counter, I saw the most interesting Christmas ornament hanging on the tree in the store window. The red glass was shaped like a heart, and a jeweled clasp held the top and bottom together. When I picked the delicate ornament up, I gently pressed the gem and the heart sprung open to reveal two smaller glass hearts nestled together inside.

When Ms. Howe appeared with a cup of cider and a candle named *Friendship*, I told her it was perfect, and hung the heart-shaped ornament back on the tree. She explained the candle had been made with orange oil and nutmeg, herbs that symbolize friendship, as she moved to the back of the store to find a bag. There was an exchange of green bills for shiny green tissue paper, and when the jingle bells on the door rang as I exited, Ruby warned that someone else had their eye on the heart ornament and if I wanted it, I'd better buy it soon.

The rest of the day was spent at the station's front desk. I made three pots of coffee to keep everyone caffeinated, Frank Hopkins at the Burger Bar reported one of the high school kids for driving off without paying for his tater tots, my mom dropped off my freshly dry cleaned tuxedo for the Cold Moon Ball, and I filed reports until the clock struck six.

After a quick wardrobe change, I picked Kat up, and we had dinner at the Fallview Tavern & Grille. Our parents, along with most of the townies, were at the community center for the traditional feast. We discussed our plans for Christmas, each with our own families, and then we walked out to my car. I drove the coolest Eddie Bauer Edition Bronco.

We waited out the crowd we knew we'd face at the ball, standing under the stars as we leaned against the Bronco. At first, we talked about the town's Christmas decorations. Then, Kat tapped on the back window, pointing out the gift bag sitting in the backseat. She was also quick to point out how the emerald green matched my bow tie and cumber bun.

I opened the door and explained the gift was for her. She said it clashed with her neon pink party dress. Mentally, I made a note it was another sign we weren't meant for each other.

Oddly enough, Kat refused the gift at first. She stuttered over her words and fidgeted with her handbag. I didn't understand until she admitted that she wanted to break up with me. She rambled about bad timing, her appreciation for our friendship, and something about a new family in town. I was shocked, but thrust the gift bag in her direction, insisting she open it. After reluctantly lifting the candle from its shiny green wrapping, she read the label wrapped around it.

Friendship.

We looked at each other knowingly, then burst into laughter. We agreed to go to the ball as friends and drove to the Mills mansion together. But once we were at the ball, she managed to find some of her friends, and we parted ways.

My ego had been bruised enough that I moped a little. Not even the rooms, glittered in red and green from floor to ceiling, could make me feel better. As others greeted me, I smiled and nodded, not really listening to their well wishes. Some people danced, others stood in small groups reminiscing about the year, and a few of us took it all in silently.

I was just minding my own business when the most beautiful woman I'd ever seen walked into the ballroom. The same way my inner wolf magically warned me about danger, the magic pulled me to her. It was a different kind of danger, because I had no idea if she'd feel the same way.

"Holy crap!" Connor exclaimed in surprise. "I didn't know you dated Joe and Boris's mom. And she totally dumped you."

Morgan patted her father's hand and said, "You always tell the story about getting engaged at Christmas, but I think this is the first time I've heard about how you guys met."

Connor laughed as he stood up from the kitchen table and made his way to the sink with an empty plate in his hands. "Now, I know why you don't tell the story."

"I bet it took you some time to get the nerve to ask Mom out," Morgan added.

Conall stood up from the table, shaking his head.

"You two don't have much faith in me, do you?" he asked as he followed behind Connor, rinsing the sticky maple syrup off his dish before setting it in the dishwasher.

"Ever since that night, I've had faith in you," Mille said with a smile. "Let's go sit in the living room, and I'll finish telling you two the story."

Once upon a time, when I was a little younger and searching for a place to call home, I found Havenwood Falls. I'd grown up in a country tainted with political unrest. I'd been raised in a wolf pack determined to arrange marriages for the sake of maintaining the pack's pure bloodline. Escaping all I knew was the only way I, or any of my family, could really have a life.

"Whoa, really?" Connor interrupted, his brows furrowed in frustration.

"Really." Millie placed her hand on her son's knee and squeezed gently. "In fact, we'd have to arrange your marriage by the time you shifted the first time."

Connor's eyes widened, and his mouth fell open.

"Luckily, for you and for me, there's more to the story," Millie said with a smile, and continued.

In the early 1980s, Northern California was my home. My family, the Casimirs, had found a way out of Europe by sneaking onto a cargo ship, and we settled into an American way of living. We all found jobs, and my younger brother even found a wife.

After a few years, I began to miss living in a larger pack. My wolf form loved the forests filled with redwoods, and I would spend days roaming the national parks free from the fear of being hunted. When I explained how I'd been feeling to my parents, they admitted they'd been struggling as well. All of us, except my married brother, agreed to find a pack. We set out on the road and headed east. Driving in the mountains, we saw a shuttle transporting tourists to a resort and followed. We had no idea we'd find a beautiful, mystical town, Havenwood Falls. Over the years since then, we've come to the conclusion that the falls magically pulled us to Colorado, which they do for those who are meant to be here.

My parents did most of the leg work, getting us approved to stay through the Court of the Sun and the Moon. We were given an informal tour by the Greg family, members of the Kasun Pack. That's when my older brother, Ivan, first met Kat. It wasn't until Kat asked if we were going to the Cold Moon Ball, that we even found out how many supernaturals lived in the town. We'd attended the feast at the community center, and the history of how wolf shifters, witches, fae, and more coexisted with each other and humans for so long gave us hope.

Our family met some of the town leaders, as well as Gaby and Ric Kasun. The female alpha did not disappoint. She asked about how we could see ourselves contributing to the community, and by the last course extended an invitation for us to stay and join the pack. Dinner ended, and as everyone began to gather their things for the ball, my family agreed to ride with the Kasuns to the Mills mansion. I needed to stop for coffee if dancing was expected.

"So you met Grandma Gaby and Grandpa Ric before you met Daddy?" Morgan asked, while bouncing on the couch.

"Yes, honey," Millie answered, and waved for Morgan to slide over to her lap. "And, if they hadn't been so kind, I might not have ever met your daddy. But I've learned there's more magic in this town than I initially gave it credit for."

Driving through Havenwood Falls alone, I remember thinking it had *heart*. The people cared about each other. While waiting for an espresso at Broastful Brews, I felt like I could belong somewhere.

When I walked into the ballroom, it was decorated like a scene in a Christmas Hallmark movie. There were glittering trees decorated around the room and lighted garland strung overhead from the chandeliers to the tops of the windows. Everyone dancing moved as if they were gliding over the hardwood floor, and cheer and laughter filled the air. Taking it all in, a peace came over me.

It didn't take long for my eyes to find a ruggedly handsome man in the corner. I was intrigued. His shaggy dark hair didn't match the perfectly tailored tuxedo, but his green bow tie did go with my red and green plaid cocktail dress, with puffy sleeves. He looked up at me as I walked in his direction, and I figured I'd try to play it cool.

My inner wolf was eager to meet the stranger, but social etiquette demanded I play hard to get. My internal struggle resulted in me walking past him, only to stop awkwardly a few feet away. Luckily, for Conall and myself, our parents saw us and walked over to make sure we were introduced to each other.

I agreed to dance when your father asked, but not only to escape from my parents' question-and-answer session with the Kasuns. My inner wolf didn't want to leave Conall's side. After we danced, I thought he might choose another woman to dance with, but he stayed by my side throughout the night. We explored a few of the rooms connected to the ballroom and talked about everything and nothing.

In the formal living room of the mansion, we sat on an ottoman in front of the Mills' fifteen-foot Christmas tree and talked for hours. A heart-shaped ornament hung at eye-level, and your father noticed that I kept glancing at it. He mentioned having seen the same ornament earlier that day, then proceeded to slip the glass heart off its limb.

He pressed the ruby clasp, and when it opened, he asked how I'd found my way into his life and his heart all in the same night. I'd felt the same way. Then he tried to hand me the ornament.

"How romantic!" Morgan jumped up and giggled. She pretended to slow dance in front of the Christmas tree.

"I agree, very romantic." Conall smiled and winked at Millie. He slid his hand into hers and pulled her up from the couch.

Connor chuckled, and said, "So the ornament you love so much, and the first gift Dad ever gave you, was stolen?"

"Oh gosh, no," Millie exclaimed. "The story isn't finished. And the ending proves your dad has always been this cheesy."

Conall wrapped his arms around her and added defensively, "I've only been this cheesy since I met you that night."

"Fine," Millie conceded. "Now let me finish."

I protested, but by the end of the night, your dad had explained to Jetta Mills that he'd seen the same ornament earlier at the Howes' shop. He promised to buy it and bring her the new ornament so he could gift the one hanging on the tree to me. He told her I was the heart of his Christmas. I don't think I've heard him say anything so cheesy since. Jetta totally fell for his romantic tale, and relinquished the ornament, clarifying she'd just bought the ornament that afternoon.

The heart-shaped ornament has been a part of every Christmas since that night. We'd found each other, our mates, and the single heart was a symbol of how we would always be one. We told our families about our magical connection two days later, our first Christmas together. Conall proposed with the heart carrying an engagement ring the next Christmas. And it hung from my wedding bouquet the following Christmas. Over the years, I've used the compartment at the heart's center to share important news, like being pregnant with each of you, with your father.

I really hate that I've lost our ornament.

"That was a great story, Momma," Morgan said as she bounced on the couch, working off the maple syrup.

Connor leaned away from her, as if her energy were contagious. "It was good, but the story of when Dad proposed is better."

"Our Christmas engagement is definitely one of my top five

favorite Christmases," Millie said as she stood up from the couch. Then she fiddled with her wedding ring. Her memories of that night had always been precious, but sharing the way she and Conall magically fell in love was also something she cherished. "This Christmas might be one of my favorites, too. If only I could find that ornament."

Conall cleared his throat, feeling a little guilty about his secret, and said, "It's not lost. I've known where it is the whole time."

"Daddy!" Morgan shamed him with a pointed finger wagging in the air. "How could you?"

Millie's eyes widened in surprise. She said, "Oh, Conall," unsure of what else to say. She didn't understand why he would have kept it from her unless the ornament was broken.

"Don't worry. It's been here the whole time. I'll show you." Conall directed them all to the tree, but instead of the ornament hanging at the top, he pulled a package out from underneath.

The box was wrapped with shimmering white paper. Conall handed it to Millie, and said, "Happy anniversary, Millie. Go ahead —open it."

He smiled, and she couldn't argue with the pure joy that exuded from him. She took her time, running her finger under the tape and unfolding the paper. Opening the box, a familiar red heart was revealed. Millie took it in her hands and pressed the jeweled clasp. When the top of the heart sprang open, a beautiful ring with two rows of diamonds, and a row of pearls set between them, was revealed.

"It's beautiful," Millie admired.

Conall moved to kneel in front of her and took her hand in his. He slipped her wedding band off her finger, then placed the new band under it. The two rings fit together perfectly.

Conall placed the rings on her finger, and said, "There are two rows of ten diamonds to represent our first twenty years of marriage, and the row of ten pearls represents the last ten years. If I have anything to say about it, we'll get to cover all of your fingers with rings because we'll have such a long life together."

"Thank you, Conall, it's perfect," she said. She took Conall's face in her hands and kissed him.

"Ew," Connor exclaimed. "Get a room!"

"This is my room," Conall responded. "In fact, every room in this house is technically mine."

"Okay, okay," Connor conceded. "That's my queue to leave."

"I think they're cute." Morgan grinned.

"What is it with the women in this family and holidays?" Connor asked, but he didn't wait for an answer before going to his room.

"You know, he'll come around eventually," Conall reasoned and pressed his lips to Millie's again.

"Oh, I know," Millie smiled. "Because he has a heart just like his father's."

Be sure to read all of the Kasun wolf pack family stories by Kallie Ross:

Written in the Stars
Defying Gravity
A Pack of Lies
Promise the Moon

WHITE WEDDING

BY KRISTIE COOK

A Moroi Vampire Christmas Story

*T*he red-headed vampire slammed her fist on the bar and shouted, "Hey, bar boy! Six more!"

Rhys Graywalk, owner of the Dirty Knuckle and a Seelie fae, lifted a dark brow at us from the other end of the bar. Sindi flashed her warmest smile, her teeth bright white against bloodred lips, and flipped her hair—nearly as red as her mouth—over her shoulder.

"Please?" she added, batting her eyelashes and practically purring.

I elbowed her in the ribs and hissed, "You know he's taken. Flirt elsewhere."

She looked at me with glassy blue eyes and pouted. "But, Michaela, you won't let me flirt with the one I want."

"Just because I'm marrying a Roca doesn't mean you need to get involved with their mess."

My second best friend who'd moved all the way from Atlanta to help me manage the inn I'd inherited—and to meet cute lumberjacks, according to her—had had her eye on the least lumberjack of them all, Adrian Roca, Xandru's younger brother, for

HAVENWOOD FALLS COLLECTIVE

a few years now. The gothic vampire was different from us moroi, but she was still plenty familiar with the bloodlust and had helped me through my transition when she'd found me just after I'd been turned. I owed her my life, and keeping her out of the Roca family was one way I tried to repay her.

Xandru was the only decent one in that family, though I supposed I could admit that Tase was at least *trying*, especially now that he had a kid. I didn't have such high hopes for the rest of their siblings. Fortunately, there had been plenty of other men to distract Sindi from making any moves on Adrian, but she was barking up the wrong tree with Rhys. He was happily together with Gwen, the tattoo artist.

Six shot glasses slid down to us from all the way at the other end, not a single drop spilling. I smiled and mouthed "thanks" to Rhys. He just shook his head and went back to talking to his more . . . subdued patrons.

Sindi handed out the shot glasses to Addie Beaumont, my first best friend and my sister from another mister, Harper Sinclair, Callie Montgomery, Sedona Matthews, and me. Then she lifted her glass in the air, tequila sloshing over her hand.

"Here's to being single, drinking doubles, and seeing triple," she toasted, slurring her words.

"This is a bachelorette party," Harper reminded her. "I'm not sure it's cool to toast to being single."

Sindi shrugged and was about to toss her shot back, but Addie stopped her.

"I got one!" she squawked, and she jumped up to stand on the bar. She held her glass up and looked down at me with a wicked glint in her eyes. "May all your ups and downs come only between the sheets!"

"Whoop, whoop!" Sindi cheered, and several people around us snickered.

Callie joined Addie on the bar. "And may you never go to bed mad. Stay up and fucking fight!"

We all laughed and lifted the glasses to our mouths—

"Wait. Wait. Wait. I have another!" Addie claimed. Her voice grew loud enough for the whole bar to hear. "Women may have

92

many faults, but men have only two—everything they say and everything they do."

All the females in the establishment cheered. Most of the men chuckled, knowing better than to protest.

"Hold on, hold on," Sindi said, climbing up on the bar too. "We can't end this night without an Irish toast." She swayed a little on her feet as she looked around, smiling devilishly before clearing her throat.

"When God made women, he made 'em outta lace.

He didn't have enough, so he left a little space.

When God made man, he made 'em out of string.

He had a little left over, so he left a little thing.

Here's to string!"

"Here's to string!" the entire crowd cheered.

The three women on the bar nearly tumbled off, they laughed so hard. Sedona, Harper, and I could barely catch them, tears streaming down our faces.

I'd lost count of how many shots we'd had. Everyone was buying them, not just for me, but for all of us. Finally, Rhys cut us off.

"Aren't you supposed to be getting your beauty sleep or something, tomorrow being your big day?" he teased.

Addie howled. "She's fucking Michaela Petran! My girl has never needed a minute of *beauty* sleep in her gods damned life. She's always gorgeous."

"Well, it's closing time," Rhys said. "Maybe none of you need beauty sleep, but I do."

"Hey, you can't complain about us too much, Greywalk," Addie chided. "You could have had the boys here instead of us."

Chuckling, he nodded. "Good point. I'm pretty sure my bar would have been destroyed. Still—you girls closed down the place. Good job. Now go home."

"Waaaait," Sindi slurred, holding up a finger. She pointed it in the general direction of Rhys, swirling it in a wobbly circle. "You forgot last call."

"Last call was nearly an hour ago," he said.

"Oh, yeah! I remember! When we made our toasts," Callie said.

"Come on, girls, it's time to go before he literally kicks us out." Harper started gathering coats from the backs of chairs and handing them out, Sedona helping her. The two were quieter than the rest of our group and hadn't drank nearly as much, which was a good thing because I never could have wrangled Addie, Callie, and Sindi out by myself. I'd quietly passed on a few shots, too, because regardless of what Addie said, I really didn't need a hangover tomorrow—my wedding day.

And it was about damn time. It'd been nearly three years since Xandru proposed, after a romantic picnic under a pile of blankets in the back of his truck on a freezing cold January night. We were supposed to be married the following Christmas Eve, but the Collector ruined those plans. We'd tried to plan other dates, but something always came up. It had been impossible to plan for last Christmas, since the Sun & Moon Academy College of Supernatural Guardians had its first semester last fall, and Addie and I were too much a part of pulling that together to be able to plan a wedding, too. This spring—after another attack by the Collector—was Aurelia's graduation, and then my sister begged me to turn her during the summer so she could test for SMA's second year of admissions. She wanted to go with her friends, not wait another year or two, so we'd done the family ceremony, and I triggered her moroi gene. All three Petran siblings were now officially vampires.

And finally, things settled down, and we could plan my Christmas Eve wedding—again. Come hell or high water, it was happening. Or a blizzard, as it was.

"Wow, looks like the storm's starting," Sedona said when we finally stumbled out of the Dirty Knuckle.

Huge, clumpy flakes fell from clouds so low, the sky looked more gray than black, though it was around two in the morning. Several inches already covered the ground, but according to the forecasts, this was barely the beginning. They were expecting at least a foot of snow overnight and more tomorrow. I looked behind us at Mount Mae, its craggy peaks lost in the clouds, the lights of the ski resort off but the slopes glowing with fresh powder, like rivers through the trees.

HAVENWOOD FALLS SHORT STORY ANTHOLOGY 2020

"The slopes are going to be so awesome tomorrow," Addie sing-songed as we half-trudged, half-stumbled through the snow, making our way toward town square.

"We have a wedding tomorrow," Sindi reminded her, and butterflies erupted in my stomach, like they always did when the words were said aloud.

"It's not until evening. We can grab a couple of hours on the slopes in the morning, right, Michaela?"

"Absolutely," I agreed. I didn't usually do mornings—I was more the nocturnal type—but I was one-hundred percent certain I wouldn't be able to sleep in tomorrow. A few runs down the mountain would hopefully help with the nerves. Not that I was anxious about getting married—I *was* anxious about it not happening at all. It still seemed unreal.

"At least you don't have to worry about breaking a leg or anything," Harper chimed in. "Unlike us mere mortals."

Harper was a psychic, a spirit writer who communicated with the other realms through the written word. She and her aunt Eloise weren't quite supernatural, but considered to be magically endowed, so they were a part of the secret side of our town. I hoped someday she and Elias, the angel, might decide to tie the knot. They made the cutest couple.

Sedona, a witch and empath, had an angel of her own—Micah, who was waiting for her outside her bookstore, Shelf Indulgence, when we turned the corner onto Main Street. Elias was there, as well, waiting on Harper. They all offered to take Callie home, which she argued about briefly, claiming there was a bed in the backroom of her store, two doors down from Shelf Indulgence, only Coffee Haven and the alley between them. The sober people won, guiding Callie into the backseat of Micah's car even as she continued mumbling protests.

"Here's to string!" Callie yelled out the window as they pulled away.

"Here's to string!" Addie, Sindi, and I all yelled back before making our way to Whisper Falls Inn, aka home, at least for Sindi and me. Addie was staying the night with me since Tase was out with his brother, having their own celebration. I tried hard not to think about what that would entail and hadn't even asked before they left this afternoon. Some things were better not known.

"Wait—we have to bless the inn for tomorrow," Addie said when we reached the back lawn of the Victorian mansion that was all mine—well, mine and my siblings'. She fell backward into the snow and started making a snow angel. Sindi and I joined her, all of us giggling as fat flakes fell in our faces and stuck in our lashes.

"Okay, the inn is blessed, we really need to get to bed," I said, standing. "Big day tomorrow." I bent over and reached for each of their hands, helping them to their feet.

"My girl's finally getting married," Addie whispered not so quietly, shoulder-bumping me as we walked toward the five cottages lining the back of the inn's property.

They'd all been damaged during the attack last May, including the one I'd been sharing with my siblings and the one Sindi lived in next door. We decided to rebuild ours a little larger because Xandru and I would continue to live here, along with Gabe, my fifteen-year-old brother. It was convenient, being on the inn's property, and I still couldn't bring myself to move into our family's estate in Havenwood Heights. Maybe once we started our own family, but not now. Not yet. I just couldn't fathom taking over the master bedroom yet—what had been my parents' room for nearly a hundred years.

"And you're next," I said to Addie after we said goodnight to Sindi.

"Hmph," she replied, and that was the last I heard from her before she stumbled into my cottage and literally crashed on the couch, out like a light.

Even with all the alcohol, I barely slept, my eyes popping wide open at nine a.m., which was practically like the ass-crack of dawn to me.

"It's Christmas Eve, and I'm getting married today," I whispered to the ceiling, a smile spreading across my face even as the butterflies danced again. I jumped out of bed and ran out into the living room. "I'm getting married today!" I shouted.

"Fuck off," Addie mumbled from under a pillow and a pile of blankets.

I grabbed the pillow off her head, fighting her for a minute before she finally gave in and let me have it.

"Can we at least have coffee first?" she muttered, squinting at me.

"Most definitely, and you should probably add a shot of your magic hangover eliminator potion juju stuff."

"No shit." She sat up and rubbed her hands over her face, then fumbled around in her coat, which hadn't made it farther than the floor next to her, extracting two vials. I probably would have been okay with a glass of blood and coffee, but figured a little extra magic wouldn't hurt. After the cobwebs seemed to clear a little, Addie sprang to her feet, grinning widely. "You're getting married today!"

We jumped up and down like we were twelve again, then danced around the living room for a while before sitting down to go over our plans for the day.

"First stop, Dress Perfect," I said as I went over the list typed into my phone. "Nina was waiting on one more piece of fabric for the final touch that she insisted on. She can do the final fitting and finish up while we do everything else. If we ski until about one or so, we'll have enough time to grab a bite to eat before we meet Sindi and Aurelia at Shear Magic for hair and makeup at two. Then back to Nina's to get our dresses at four and to the inn to get ready!" I might have squealed the last part with a little extra enthusiasm. I was especially glad we'd finished decorating the ballroom yesterday so we wouldn't have to worry about a thing at the inn.

"Correction," Addie said. "First stop is Coffee Haven."

"Oh, of course. That was implied."

After another half hour or so of going over everything one more time, we grabbed our coats and shoved them on while throwing the door open—to nearly two feet of snow that tumbled into the cottage.

"Holy shit," Addie said as she tugged her beanie hat on.

"Right. Snowstorm. Kind of forgot about that," I muttered as I began mentally reviewing the schedule one more time, making tweaks to allow for the snow, while Addie muttered a spell that cleared the mess in my doorway.

The flakes came down heavily in streaks of white, the clouds still low and dark, showing no signs of letting up anytime soon. The wind whipped and howled, blowing snow sideways, and I could barely see any of the buildings of town square just beyond the inn.

"Definitely our biggest storm yet this year," Addie said.

"It's perfect!" I said with a grin. Most brides would think me crazy, but I couldn't have asked for more perfect weather for my wedding day.

Zipping our coats up and pulling our hats down further over our ears just to cross the back lawn, we put our heads down and pushed through to reach the backside of the inn. All three sets of French doors *and* the conservatory were locked, though—of course, they were, because they led straight into the dining room-slash-ballroom, and absolutely nobody was allowed in until it was time, not even me and especially not with snow-packed boots. So we trudged to the next closest door, the one into the kitchen near the far corner of the building. The door practically flew off its hinges when we opened it, and everyone stopped in mid-action to stare at us as we hurried in.

"Shut the damn door!" Chef yelled.

"Sorry!" I shouted, yanking it closed.

"Oh, sorry, boss," she called from the other end of the kitchen. "I didn't realize it was you."

"I'd be yelling, too," I said. "It's cold out there."

We stomped the snow off our feet in the small vestibule, using towels to dry our wet boots as much as possible so we didn't create a hazard as we traipsed through the kitchen. We slipped through the door that connected to the back offices, then kicked said boots off before heading out to the lobby.

Aurelia, home from college for the break, stood behind the front desk, and her dark brows pinched together when she saw us. My breath still caught at the sight of her greenish-gray moroi eyes, after nearly nineteen years of them being normal, human brown.

"Didn't expect you up so early," she said, "considering how you both stumb—"

"Shh!" I hushed, tilting my head toward the guests gathered in the front parlor.

She dropped her voice to a whisper only us supernaturals could hear. "Considering how messed up you both were last night when you got home—and loud as hell, by the way."

"Psh, I'm pretty sure I passed out the moment I was inside," Addie said. "I barely remember getting home."

Aurelia laughed and shook her dark head. "I can't believe I missed all the fun. You should have let me come."

"You're underage," I reminded her. "So how are things going?"

"Well . . ." She cringed, gnawing on her bottom lip. I knew that look—it had become very familiar during her last two years of high school. There was something she really didn't want to tell me.

And on this day, I was pretty sure I didn't want to hear it. "Do I want to know?"

"Probably not, but . . ." She trailed off, leaving us hanging.

"Ugh. Just spit it out," Addie said, rubbing her temple.

Aurelia's gaze slid to the front of the inn, staring out the glass door toward town square. In just the few minutes since we'd left the cottage, it seemed the storm had worsened, becoming a near whiteout. I couldn't even see the gazebo or trees of Town Square Park across the street, or the sides of Simple Treasures Pawn Shop or Hey! Nice Glass!, the two buildings closest to us.

Seemingly stepping out of nowhere, Sindi burst through the front door at that moment, carrying a large tray of Coffee Haven to-go cups.

"Gah! Why did I move here again?" she demanded as she blinked snowflakes out of her eyes, her gaze catching mine. "Oh, good, you're up and you don't look too worse for the wear," she said, placing the tray on the counter and handing Addie and me each a cup. "So, I have good news and good news, and also bad news, more bad news and . . . really bad news."

I took a sip of delicious coffee, staring at her over the rim. Only a vampire could look so bright and cheery after how much she'd drank last night. Her red hair was pulled up in a high ponytail, and as usual, her full lips were painted just as red, making her blue eyes pop.

"Good news first," she said when I didn't reply. "You have your Winter Wonderland for your wedding!"

The cheerful glee she said it with was so opposite her normal sarcastic demeanor, my suspicion grew—along with a sick feeling in my stomach. No longer did butterflies dance. No, now there were snakes in there, coiling and slithering, forming a big undulating knot.

"You think?" Addie asked when I still didn't say anything.

Sindi gave a weak smile.

"And the other good news?" I prodded.

"Coffee Haven is open . . . but I don't know for how much longer. I was able to snag us some coffee, though."

"And we thank you very much for that," I said, holding my cup in both hands, although I wasn't sure I could drink another sip as dread continued to fill me.

"What's the rest?" Addie asked on a sigh. "Just get it out so we can deal with it."

"Well, the first bad news: you won't be able to go skiing because the lifts just closed due to the whiteout conditions."

We both nodded, not surprised at this. I'd already come to the conclusion by the time we crossed the lawn.

"Tase said he might have to close them if it got as bad as they said it would," Addie said. "And it obviously did. Worse, maybe."

Sindi cringed, and Aurelia backed away behind her, ducking out from behind the desk to make herself scarce. That wasn't good —Aurelia loved drama.

"Tase didn't make the call," Sindi said. "Seamus, the new guy, did. He's the only one . . . around."

Addie and I exchanged a look.

"What does that mean?" I asked, my words slow and heavy. A big bomb was coming, I just knew.

"Well, the second bad news—Burdorf Pass is closed and will probably be closed all day and possibly into tomorrow, according to Rusty, who's been patrolling all night."

I glanced at the people in the parlor and said quietly, "We have guests who are supposed to be checking out, though. We need the space for tonight."

We'd reserved rooms for our wedding party and close friends as a special thank-you treat and also so they wouldn't have to drive home, which meant they could party harder.

"Yeah, well, not really anything we can do about it."

The knot of snakes tightened, but I nodded. "Yeah, right, of course. I mean, unless the Luna Coven can do something?"

I looked over at Addie with a shred of hope, not just for the wedding but for the tourists who'd planned to be home for Christmas tomorrow.

"You know better than that," she whispered. "Even if we could magically make that much snow disappear, they'll just get trapped farther down the highway. We can't clear the roads all the way to Grand Junction without raising suspicion. Not in a storm like this."

"Not that it would matter," Sindi said. "The interstate is closed, all the airports, everything." She looked over at the guests. "They already know, Kaela. They'll be staying."

I blew out a sigh. "Okay, no worries. We'll figure it out. I'm not going to let that ruin my day."

Sindi didn't reply, but I could tell there was more.

"And the really bad news?" Addie urged, also sensing that Sindi wasn't done.

The big bomb—it was coming. Right now.

"Xandru, Tase, and Adrian went to Telluride last night," she said, her words fast and quiet as though she had to force them off her tongue before she chickened out.

"And . . . ?"

She tilted her head, lifting her brows. "And . . . the roads are closed?"

I stared at her for a long moment as I tried to process her meaning, my brain refusing to believe it. "Please tell me you're not saying my fiancé—my fucking *groom*—is stuck out of town on my. Wedding. Day!"

When she didn't answer, Addie and I were both on our phones, calling Xandru and Tase. We both got voicemail. Both males were given very demanding orders to call immediately. As soon as I finished with the recording, I tried again.

"*We're sorry. Our network is experiencing technical difficulties. Please try again later.*"

I absently pressed the End button, my breaths coming quick

and my stomach dropping as panic began to set in. "No. No, no, no. This can't be happening. It really cannot be happening. Holy shit. What am I going to do?"

My voice rose with each word, all the guests turning to stare at me. Addie ushered me to the back offices before I made a very unprofessional scene.

"We'll figure something out," she said as she guided me into my own office and sat me down in the chair closest to the door.

I nodded. "Right. We have to. We can. We're a town full of magic. Surely something can be done. Right? Please, Addie, tell me something can be done! I can't get married without a fucking groom!"

"I'll, uh, I'll make some calls." She sat in my chair behind the desk and pulled out her phone—the special one for Court members only. I appreciated her efforts, but I could hear the lack of confidence in her voice, more and more with each phone call.

The longer I sat in that chair watching Addie call Court members and Luna members and even the human city council, the more freaked out I grew. Anger and disbelief chased each other. Xandru had left town when he knew a major snowstorm was coming in. How could he be so stupid? No, he wasn't stupid. I couldn't believe he would take such a risk. It had to have been his brothers.

"I'm going to kill Tase," I murmured, my first words in over an hour, my hands wringing in my lap as I pictured his neck between them. "This has to be all him."

"I don't know. My bet's on Adrian," Addie said, setting her phone on the desk. I lifted a brow, glaring at her. She held her hands up, palms out. "I know Tase can be an idiot sometimes. Trust me, I know better than anyone. But he wouldn't have purposely done anything that could remotely piss you off, Kales. You're one of the few people he respects, and he has *mad* respect for you. He wouldn't have risked this on your wedding day. Adrian, on the other hand . . . he's young and has no experience with a real relationship. He'd be more likely to want to do something more than the same ol'-same ol' for his big brother's bachelor party."

"Ugh!" I shoved my hands through my hair. "Why the hell did

they go all the way to Telluride, though? Why couldn't they have just gone to Silk? Is that not special enough for them?"

Silk was our town's only swanky nightclub, housed in a series of caves and old mines in Miles Mountain on the western edge of town. Addie's aunt on her hellhound side owned it. We rarely ever went out there, the cover charge and cost of drinks way beyond our budget, even for a special occasion like my bachelorette party. Tase could have afforded it, though. Why hadn't that been good enough?

"Who knows? They're all just stupid boys sometimes."

I couldn't argue with that. "What am I going to do, Addie?"

Tears pricked the backs of my eyes, and I tried to blink them away, but was starting to lose that fight, my sight blurring.

"I mean, they are vampires. Telluride's not that far the way the crow flies, and they know the back country better than most. If anyone can find a way in, it's them. They just need a little extra time."

Squeezing my eyes shut, I nodded. After some deep cleansing breaths, I whispered, "He'll make it. Xandru wants this just as much as I do. He'll find a way. I have to trust that he will."

I was just beginning to calm down when my phone rang.

"Xandru?" I answered without looking at the screen.

"Michaela?" asked a female voice with an Italian accent.

Damn. "Nina?"

"Yes, it is me. I . . . I'm sorry, Michaela, but the fabric I ordered was supposed to arrive first thing this morning so I could finish your dress. CDI called last night, though, because their delivery truck went into the ditch outside of Montrose."

"Of course it did," I muttered, sinking lower in my chair.

"Mat and I drove up here to get it, but—"

"But now you're snowed in in Montrose," I finished for her. Addie's brows rose.

"I'm so sorry, Michaela," Nina said, sincere remorse filling her tone. "I'll do my best to get back in time."

I might have been in shock or something at this point, because I felt nothing at the news that my dream wedding dress would not —and could not—be finished and here in time. I should have known to stick with the original design, but when Nina had been struck with inspiration a couple of weeks ago and shown me the sketch, it was like she'd finally captured the image in my own mind perfectly—actually even better than I'd been able to imagine. I'd tried to talk myself out of taking the risk, but I just couldn't. And here we were.

But what good would the dress be when there was still no groom?

"Don't worry. Just please be safe," I told Nina, numbly disconnecting the call just when there was a knock on the door.

Sindi slipped inside. "We have another problem, and this one's really bad. You know the Nixons and the Wakefields?"

Rubbing my temples, I nodded. "The big extended family occupying six of our rooms? Of course."

"Well, the two teenaged boys—the cousins? They left at dawn to go snowboarding. And nobody's heard from them since. The parents have been trying to call them ever since they heard us say the lifts had been closed."

All thoughts of the wedding vanished.

The three of us jumped on our phones, calling Court members and Sheriff Ric Kasun. Within minutes, a large crowd filled the first floor of the inn to bursting, maps laid out on the front desk and in the parlor as search teams divvied up and made plans. The family spoke with the locals about what runs and trails they'd mostly been skiing all week.

"They're our best snowboarders, though," Mrs. Wakefield said. "They wanted to try some of the backside slopes. That's why they left so early—to make the hike to Asher's 50."

Addie and I exchanged a look. The runs on the backside of Mount Mae were some of the most challenging in the state of Colorado, with cornices, cliffs, and some of the steepest pitches this end of the Rockies. Asher's 50 was the biggest bitch of them all, way beyond a double black diamond, named for its fifty-degree pitch. Just to get to it required a thirty-minute hike from the closest lift. Even on good weather days, hardly anyone went over to that area. On a day like today? They'd be all alone. Nobody else to come across them. And the way the snow was blowing, it might be impossible to find them—if they weren't already buried.

"You stay here and keep the family calm," Addie said to me as the search groups prepared to head out. "And maybe Xandru or Tase will finally get a call through, too. It would be great if they could—they know the backside better than anyone."

I nodded. Even though Addie and I knew those runs fairly well, I was in no shape to help the search team. I wasn't sure I was in any shape to help the families, though, either.

"Be safe," I told her as I hugged her, not wanting to let go. Afraid more bad news would come, this time involving her. At least she'd be accompanied by another witch and a couple of shifters in her group, and no humans, which meant they could use their supernatural abilities. That would hopefully give them an edge.

The inn felt empty and sad once everyone left. Well, not everyone, of course. Sheriff Kasun had somehow convinced the family members to stay behind because the conditions were too dangerous out on the mountain. They were all gathered together in the front parlor, consoling each other. I was about to alert the kitchen to adapt our dinner plans when the front door blew open again and Willow, Harper, Sedona, and a slew of other people came in, carrying urns of coffee and hot cocoa, pastries, and other goodies.

Sedona gathered the younger siblings and other kids in the library and sat them down for story time, a nice distraction. Willow, owner of Coffee Haven and a fae with empath abilities, served food and drinks, then sat between the two mothers, holding their hands. What they didn't know was that she was taking in some of their pain and sadness, providing a bit of relief.

As the hours passed, more people came and went, some bringing more food, knowing our kitchen was currently stocked and prepped for a wedding feast, not for comfort and convenience. Others came to check in and left again to relieve some of the search parties, who returned to warm up and eat. With Gabe's help— Sindi and Aurelia had gone out with search teams—I coordinated all of the activities, making sure everyone had what they needed. As a Court member, I was also constantly answering calls to give or receive updates and making my own calls in between, but still unable to reach any of the Roca brothers. Their younger siblings hadn't heard from them, either.

Throughout the afternoon, the snowfall rate eventually slowed, the sky lightening some. But it wouldn't be for long, as evening was quickly approaching. Which meant the start of my wedding was quickly approaching—and would come and go just like all the other attempts.

When there was a lull, I drifted away from the front desk, to the ballroom, opening the door but not daring to walk in. I leaned against the doorjamb and just stared at the beauty of it all. Green garland crossed the high ceiling along the beams and crawled down the chains of the chandeliers. An archway of greenery dotted with bright red berries and flowers stood at the far end of the room, the altar we would never stand under. Small Christmas trees with red, gold, and silver ornaments served as centerpieces on the tables, and red and white poinsettias were grouped together in elaborate displays in the room's corners. White candles in silver and gold holders were scattered throughout the room, and of course, twinkle lights glittered from every possible place we could put them. Every detail had been planned and executed with my mother in mind. She loved Christmas, especially Christmas romances, and I could almost feel her with me.

"It's perfectly beautiful," Mammie said, suddenly appearing beside me, making me jump. My aunt Luiza, our resident ghost, still managed to startle me nearly every time she decided to make herself seen.

"And such a waste," I muttered, blinking away tears.

"Oh, my sweet girl, don't give up yet."

I tilted my head toward her, an ache in my chest because I just wanted a hug from my mom, but Mammie would have been the next best thing. Unfortunately, it required more energy to provide that physical comfort than she was able to give anymore. She'd even cut way down on teasing sexy males over the last few months, saving her energy for a select few she deemed worthy.

"I can't even think about it being possible right now, Mammie. I'm going to believe Xandru will eventually show up, but there are two families out there who could possibly be facing the worst news a parent could ever hear. Their needs are way more important right now."

"Of course they are. And I am so proud of you for the way you're handling all of this. But don't give up hope, darling. Christmas is a magical time. Miracles do really happen." Her ghostly form smiled, and she held her arms out before wrapping them around me. For the briefest moment, I could feel a bit of solidity to them.

"You and my mom and your Christmas romances," I teased, swiping at the tears that managed to spill over.

"You know you love them, too. And you know anything is possible."

"Thanks, Mammie. Our town is magical all of the time, not only at Christmas, but that still isn't enough. Let's just hope they find those boys. That and everyone coming home safely would be the best Christmas miracle of all."

We walked out of the ballroom—well, I walked and Mammie drifted, stopping in the doorway before any of the human guests could see her, since now was not the time to be haunting them.

"There's the Christmas spirit," she said before she disappeared, and I closed the door.

At first, I thought she referred to my comment, but then I noticed what she'd seen: local Havenwoodies gathering around two scared and distraught families, doing whatever needed to be done to support and provide comfort. From serving them food and keeping them distracted with conversation and entertainment to risking their own lives in the worst blizzard of the decade to save two young men whose lives were only beginning—my people came together to help strangers.

Before returning to the front of the house, I ducked back to the kitchen and notified the staff that dinner plans had changed.

"If you're cool with it, we can still put out the buffet," Chef said. "Just not quite so festive and beautiful as we'd planned, but more functional."

I nodded. "That will be perfect. We'll have a lot of mouths to feed over the next few hours."

"We'll have your wedding soon enough, boss," she said. "Don't worry, okay?"

I forced a smile and waved a hand in the air. "Trust me—that's the least of my worries right now."

Returning to the front, I noticed nightfall had already come. This wasn't good at all, although at least we had search teams with excellent night vision and other senses that would help. Of course, our guests didn't know that. The emotional stress was weighing heavily on everyone here at the inn, as there'd been no news for so long.

"There will be food in the ballroom in a few minutes for anyone who's hungry," I announced lamely, thinking nobody would have much desire for food. To my surprise, though, the front rooms nearly cleared out as they headed back to the ballroom.

"It smells too mouthwatering to pass up," one of the uncles or cousins or whatever said as he passed by.

"Oh, honey, this was supposed to be your wedding reception, wasn't it?" Mrs. Nixon said, grabbing my hands as she came up next to me. Her eyes were puffy and red from crying all day. "I'm so sorry."

"*You're* sorry?" I said in disbelief. "Oh, Mrs. Nixon, please. I'm not worried about it, and you most definitely don't need to be." I slid an arm over her shoulder. "We're going to put all of our energy into believing your son and nephew are going to walk through that door with the story of a lifetime."

She nodded and smiled weakly before more tears began flowing. I pulled her into a hug, while sending out those positive vibes like Addie was always preaching to me. She eventually let me go, claiming she was hungry, but as I watched, I noticed how she only pushed her food around on her plate.

A commotion behind me had me whirling toward the front door, and my jaw dropped as people began pouring into the lobby, chatting jovially, filled with excitement. For a moment, I was about to remind them the wedding was called off when I realized who they were. The search teams! They were all returning and in good moods. That could only mean . . .

"Jack!" Mrs. Nixon screamed from behind me, nearly bowling

me over when she ran for one of the two teenaged boys who'd just come through the front door.

"Jeremiah!" Mrs. Wakefield was right on her sister-in-law's heels.

I could no longer hold back the tears as I watched their reunion, and then especially when I saw Addie come in . . . followed by two tall and broad men who looked almost like twins with dark hair curling under their snow-crusted hats and those all too familiar moroi eyes—

"Oh, my god!" I gasped, and now it was my turn to shove people out of the way. Xandru swept me up in his arms, burying his face in my neck as I held onto him like I'd never let go. "I was so worried. So, so worried. For all of you."

"I'm sorry, love. I really am."

"You should be!" I shoved my hands against his chest, breaking the embrace as anger replaced my momentary relief. So much that I forgot we were surrounded by a growing crowd. "What the hell had you been thinking, leaving town on the worst night *ever* to be leaving town! And where the hell have you been all this time where you couldn't even call? Don't tell me—your phone died or you lost it. What kind of excuse are you going to throw at me, huh?" Without letting him answer, I rounded on Tase, jabbing my finger at him. "And you! What kind of best man goes out of his way to ruin his brother's wedding? How could you have let this happen?"

"Kales," Addie said, sliding between me and the guys to catch my attention, "Xandru and Tase found the boys."

My mouth gaped open and closed several times like a fish out of water. The anger drained as fast as it had come, my whole body deflating. "You did?"

"We were on our way home, but as soon as we heard about them, we went straight to Asher's 50," Xandru said. "You know there's no good reception out there, babe."

"It took us a while, but we found them in a ravine halfway down the mountain," Tase added.

"After they got us out, we had to hike back up the mountain until one of the teams on ATVs finally found us," Jack said.

Their story and the boys' tale were repeated several more times as more people came in, details piling on with each retelling. The crowd shifted into the ballroom, devouring the food in good cheer and making all kinds of grateful toasts. It wasn't my dream wedding, but the night had become full of just as much love and friendship. As exhausted as we all were after such a harrowing day, it was after ten p.m. before we finally said goodnight to the last person.

Xandru and I stood in the ballroom as Mammie and I had earlier, admiring what was still a beautifully romantic scene. The place settings were all cleared, but all the decorations remained.

"I'm sorry, love," he said for the fiftieth time in the last hour, squeezing my hand. "We can still make it happen."

I blew out a heavy breath. "Right now, I just want my jammies, a blanket, spiked cocoa, and my favorite Christmas movie. I'll think about the wedding later. Let's just have a nice Christmas now, okay?"

He slipped his arm around my waste and pulled me into him. "As long as we're together and warm, that's all that matters."

We had just settled on the couch with Aurelia and Gabe, hot cocoas spiked with both blood and bourbon in hand and *It's a Wonderful Life* set to start, when Aurelia's phone chimed with a text message.

"Uh, I forgot something at the inn." She jumped to her feet and ran out the door, barely pausing long enough to put her boots on. "Gabe, I need help," she called as an afterthought.

"What? No," he whined.

She gave him the look—the I'm-the-big-sister-so-don't-argue-with-me look she might have learned from me. "Yes. Hurry!"

He moaned and groaned as he put his own boots on and followed her out the door.

Xandru and I snuggled under the blanket, waiting patiently . . . for a while. I finally reached for my own phone to text them when it buzzed as I grabbed it.

Sindi: We need you both in the lobby pronto
Me: Seriously? I'm in my pjs ready for bed

Sindi: So what? Get your asses over here!

Me: What can't wait? And don't you dare be giving me more bad news. Had enough for today

Sindi: Just get over here. I promise it will be worth it

"Ugh. They're up to something," I said, standing and pulling on Xandru's hands.

Not bothering to change out of our matching Christmas-themed pajamas, we shoved our feet into boots, grabbed our coats, and trudged back across the lawn to the inn. The kitchen was dark and quiet, the staff probably at home, warm in their beds or by the fire. We found Sindi and my siblings in the lobby, but glancing around, I noticed nothing demanding her urgency.

"What's going on?" I asked. She looked us both up and down and frowned. "Hey, no judging. I told you we were in our jammies. Besides, you're not any better."

She, too, was in Christmas pajamas, the ones I'd bought for her, decorated with sloths wearing a Santa hat. I'd never thought in a million years she'd wear them, though, since she slept nude, and definitely never in public.

She shook her head, red locks flying, then went around the front desk and reached down to the shelves under it. "Take your coats and boots off. And here. Put these on."

She set two pairs of complimentary slippers on the desk, the Whisper Falls Inn logo embroidered in silver on the tops. I opened my mouth to protest.

"Just do it!" she insisted. "Okay, Aurelia and Gabe, get in position. Addie, we're ready!"

I cocked my head. I thought Addie had gone home a long time ago for her own mini-reunion with Tase. She came around the corner, decked out in red-and-black flannel pajama pants and a black long-sleeve top with an image of Christmas ornaments and the words, "I like your balls" in metallic silver. She held a bouquet in her hands, grinning at me.

"What's going on?" I asked again.

"Here," Sindi said, shoving my own bouquet at me—white chrysanthemums with sprigs of rosemary, boxwood, pine, and red berries for color, tied with a silver ribbon.

I shook my head, the word *No* on the tip of my tongue.

"We're doing this," she said before I could protest.

At that moment, music floated from the ballroom, and I realized Gabe had opened the door.

"Come on, Xandru," he said. Xandru winked at me before following my brother in.

Aurelia strode up to the doorway, watching them, and I realized she held her bouquet, too. She looked over her shoulder at me and gave me a genuine grin, then began her stride down the aisle. As Addie prepared for her turn, Sindi came up next to me and linked her arm around mine.

"I can't believe you did this," I whispered.

"Oh, it wasn't me. Everyone made it happen. You deserve it, Kaekae." The music changed, our cue. "Now let's finally get you married."

Sindi walked me down the aisle on one arm, and Mammie joined me on the other, the two of them giving me away to my childhood sweetheart and my soulmate.

We'd known each other forever, the best of friends since birth. We'd had our ups and downs, and not just between the sheets, as Addie had wished for us, but we'd finally made it. Everyone—and I mean everyone, half the town must have been present as well as all of the inn's guests—was dressed in sleepwear. It wasn't at all what I'd dreamt about for so long, but it was the most perfect Christmas Eve wedding I could have never planned.

"Xandru and Michaela, I now pronounce you husband and wife," Mayor Barbie Stewart, wearing a flowered flannel nightgown, declared just as the church bells in the distance rang in midnight. "You may kiss your bride."

Xandru leaned in, I pushed up on my toes, and our gazes locked before our lips did. And I saw in those eyes I loved so much —the eyes that saved me when I'd been lost in another life in Atlanta—I saw in those beautiful piercing eyes all the love I would ever need.

"Merry Christmas, Mrs. Roca," he whispered.

"Merry Christmas, Mr. Petran," I said with a grin before he crashed his mouth over mine.

*MERRY CHRISTMAS AND HAPPY HOLIDAYS FROM THE
HAVENWOOD FALLS FAMILY!*

Stay up to date at www.HavenwoodFalls.com

Subscribe to our reader group and receive free stories and more!

www.ingramcontent.com/pod-product-compliance
Lightning Source LLC
Chambersburg PA
CBHW050903180626
46814CB00007B/2866